P9-CDI-849

"Think of your niece and nephew, Nicholas," Carly offered softly.

When she'd first met him two years ago, he hadn't had the children. His wife and sister had been alive. She'd seen pictures of the kids and he'd told her about each one in detail like the doting uncle he was.

Since then a lot had happened. He'd lost two women he'd loved, gained two children—and released a killer to kill again.

She blinked that thought away.

He blew out a breath and undid the buttons on his cuffs. Forearms roped with strength emerged as he shoved the sleeves up to his elbows—Carly swallowed hard desperately trying to convince herself she was *not* feeling another tug of attraction.

What was wrong with her?

Books by Lynette Eason

Love Inspired Suspense

Lethal Deception
River of Secrets
Holiday Illusion
A Silent Terror
A Silent Fury
A Silent Pursuit
Protective Custody

LYNETTE EASON

grew up in Greenville, SC. Her home church, Northgate Baptist, had a tremendous influence on her during her early years. She credits Christian parents and dedicated Sunday School teachers for her acceptance of Christ at the tender age of eight. Even as a young girl, she knew she wanted her life to reflect the love of Jesus.

Lynette attended the University of South Carolina in Columbia, SC, then moved to Spartanburg, SC, to attend Converse College, where she obtained her master's degree in education. During that time, she met the boy next door, Jack Eason, and married him. Jack is the executive director of the Sound of Light Ministries. Lynette and Jack have two precious children: Lauryn and Will. She and Jack are members of New Life Baptist Fellowship Church in Boiling Springs, SC, where Jack serves as the worship leader and Lynette teaches Sunday School to the four- and five-year-olds.

Protective Custody

LYNETTE EASON

Steeple
Hill®

Published by Steeple Hill Books™

If you purchased this book without a cover you should be aware
that this book is stolen property. It was reported as "unsold and
destroyed" to the publisher, and neither the author nor the
publisher has received any payment for this "stripped book."

STEEPLE HILL BOOKS

Steeple
Hill®

Recycling programs
for this product may
not exist in your area.

ISBN-13: 978-0-373-44405-2

PROTECTIVE CUSTODY

Copyright © 2010 by Lynette Eason

All rights reserved. Except for use in any review, the reproduction
or utilization of this work in whole or in part in any form by any
electronic, mechanical or other means, now known or hereafter
invented, including xerography, photocopying and recording, or in
any information storage or retrieval system, is forbidden without
the written permission of the editorial office, Steeple Hill Books,
233 Broadway, New York, NY 10279 U.S.A.

This is a work of fiction. Names, characters, places and incidents are
either the product of the author's imagination or are used fictitiously, and
any resemblance to actual persons, living or dead, business establishments,
events or locales is entirely coincidental.

This edition published by arrangement with Steeple Hill Books.

® and TM are trademarks of Steeple Hill Books, used under license.
Trademarks indicated with ® are registered in the United States Patent
and Trademark Office, the Canadian Trade Marks Office and in other
countries.

www.SteepleHill.com

Printed in U.S.A.

For in the day of trouble he will keep me safe in his dwelling; he will hide me in the shelter of his tabernacle and set me high upon a rock.
—*Psalms* 27:5

To my Lord and Savior who keeps me safe
and secure during the storms of life.

And to a young man who wanted to see his name
in a book. Here ya go, Nick.

ONE

In the downtown courthouse, Deputy U.S. Marshal Carly Masterson eyed the three bloody fingerprints on the cracked door and pulled her weapon.

Blood on the door to the judge's chambers.

Not a good sign.

Her partner, Mason Stone, followed her actions. In a low whisper, he asked, "Is he in there?"

Heart picking up speed, Carly toed the door open. Without a sound, it opened inward, exposing Judge Nicholas Floyd's chambers. "Nick?" She kept her voice low.

No answer.

They'd been on the way to the courthouse when they'd gotten a call that the judge had received the second threat of the day. This time the authorities were sending protection whether he wanted it or not. Three minutes later, Carly and Mason arrived to find themselves in this situation.

A sweep of the room showed nothing amiss.

Except for a few drops of blood trailing across the floor.

So where was the judge?

Anxiety twisting her stomach into knots, Carly said, "I'll take the bathroom." She headed for the closed door. "The drops of blood are fresh."

"Look at the shape of the drops. They're leading from the bathroom," he noted in a matching whisper.

She could feel her heart thudding in her chest. Her fingers reached for the knob then pulled back. "Blood on the knob."

"Noted. I've got your back."

She knew he would. Having been partners for two years, she trusted Mason with her life.

"Here." He thrust a tissue he'd retrieved from the desk into her hand. Standing to one side of the door, with Mason on the opposite side facing her, she placed the tissue over the knob, nodded to him and twisted her wrist. The door flew open at her shove, and they rounded the edges of the door frame as one, guns pointed inside.

Empty.

The bathroom contents lay scattered. Water tinged with red filled the plugged sink.

Adrenaline rushing, Carly pulled back and let the thudding in her chest subside.

Mason looked at her. "Now what?"

"We follow the blood."

Nicholas pressed his fingers to the cut and bit back a word he hadn't said in a long time. "Did you have to barge in while I was shaving? You could have at least let me grab a towel." He swiped the blood on his pants, not caring if it left a stain. That was the least of his problems right now.

The marshal simply looked at him. He'd been in the Spartanburg, South Carolina, courthouse delivering a captured fugitive to his hearing when Nick had called the authorities. The first threat had come in the form of a phone call. Nick had hung up on the caller. The letter that had appeared on his desk an hour later had been harder to ignore.

He stomped to the table and yanked a napkin from the holder. The small break room/kitchen now served as his safe area until more help arrived.

"Sorry." An unexpected apology from the man.

Pressing the napkin to the still-seeping cut, Nicholas paused. "Aw, it's all right." He'd been on his last upward stroke when the pounding on his bathroom door had caused him to jerk like he'd been shot. As a result, he'd pressed and yanked on the razor, cutting himself pretty bad.

"Want me to take a look at it?" Concern flickered on the marshal's face.

"No. It's slowing down."

The marshal shook his head and asked, "Who still uses a straight razor these days? You got something against an electric one?"

"It was my grandfather's. He taught me to use it and..." He shrugged and blushed. "I like a close shave."

"Huh. Not that close, I'm guessing."

Nick tossed the paper into the trash and grabbed another one. "You're right about that." He winced at the sting. "What's your name?"

"Seth McCoy."

"Thanks for responding so quickly, Deputy Marshal McCoy."

For the first time, a hint of a smile creased the corners of the man's eyes. "No problem. When a judge gets a letter like that, we don't waste time."

Nick grunted. "I noticed."

McCoy's eyes shifted as he raised a hand to the earpiece then spoke to the wall. "I got him. We're in the break area. One way in, one way out." A pause. "I'll be waiting."

"Who was that?"

"Your protection detail."

"Protection detail, huh?"

"Yeah, and this time you're not running them off."

Two weeks ago, marshals had been assigned to Nicholas after the first death threat, a phone call warning him to recuse himself from the de Lugo trial or to be watching his back. Nicholas had insisted it was hoax, just like the one two years ago. The marshals had reluctantly left him alone.

Now he wasn't so sure. The tone of this letter had been different. It had shaken him because it had mentioned the children. Twelve-year-old Lindsey and seven-year-old Christopher. When Nick's sister had been killed in a car wreck, he'd become their guardian. "Do you have someone on my house? On the kids' school?"

"Even as we speak."

He didn't like the feeling of relief. That meant he might actually be worried someone was serious about hurting him or the children. At least the children hadn't been threatened directly. Still, Nicholas didn't like the fact that they were mentioned—by name. "Tell them not to let the kids know anything is wrong. They've had so much turmoil in their lives. The less they know, the better. At least as long as we can leave it that way."

Again, Seth eyed him patiently. "They're professionals. The kids will be fine—and alive."

Before Nicholas could respond, a knock on the door sounded, and he flashed back to two years ago when another knock had jerked him out of his comfort zone and forced him to admit his marriage needed help.

God, please don't let it be...

"Hello, Nicholas."

...Carly Masterson.

* * *

Staring at the man before her, who was dressed in jeans and a white oxford shirt stained with blood, Carly felt a surge of attraction mixed with disdain.

To cover her shock, consternation and anger with herself at the blindsiding emotions, she moved aside to let Mason in. If she was going to be attracted to someone, why couldn't it be her partner? Unfortunately, even though she thought he was a good-looking man, Mason didn't send a single zip up her spine.

Not like the judge standing in front of her. *A judge who let a killer get off scot-free. Free to kill again. Free to kill my beloved mentor, Hank Bentley.*

Of all the assignments I could have gotten, I pulled this one. Why? Who she was appealing to, she didn't know. But it sure wasn't God. They weren't on speaking terms.

Focus, Carly. Do your job.

Derailing her unprofessional thoughts, she glanced at McCoy. "Took you long enough to let us know you had him."

McCoy raised a brow and shrugged. "You know the procedure as well as I do. Get the subject safe then report in as soon as possible. That's what I did."

Carly did know the procedure and inwardly cringed at the gentle reprimand from her peer. She was being entirely too sensitive about this...and she knew why.

Because it was Nicholas Floyd. A man she'd come to think of as a friend two years ago when she was assigned to him and his wife. A man she once admired and respected. Only to have him turn around and let a killer go on a "technicality" six months ago. She despised the word. There should be no "technicalities" in her line of work.

But Judge Floyd was also a man who was now in danger. She would put her personal feelings aside and do her job.

"Right." Turning to Nicholas, she asked, "What happened? We found blood in your office."

A flush covered his cheekbones, and he shot a look at Seth. "He surprised me while I was shaving."

Frowning, she eyed the cut on his face. "Do you need a doctor?"

"No." His lips tightened. "I need to make sure my niece and nephew are safe, then get out there in the courtroom and try the case I've got waiting for me."

"They're safe," she assured him. "As soon as we got the call, two other marshals and several officers headed for your house. Authorities are also fanning out around the building here. We're pulling the security videos from the cameras around your office."

Nick nodded. "It didn't come through the U.S. mail. It came through interoffice mail. If you look at the cameras, all you're going to see is my secretary entering my office and placing an interoffice envelope on my desk."

"We'll still check. We'll be checking your phone records, too."

Nick shook his head. "Of course, but what do you want to bet that threatening call came from an untraceable prepaid cell-phone number?"

"Unfortunately, you're probably right."

Mason cleared his throat. "What exactly did the letter say?"

Nick reached into his back pocket and pulled out a piece of paper encased in a paper bag. At Carly's raised brow, he shrugged. "I've had police training, remember? Before I decided what I wanted to do with my life, I went through the police academy. I can gather evidence without contaminating it just as well as any cop."

As she took it from him, her fingers brushed his and she felt their warmth briefly against her own. Shivers danced along her spine and she cleared her throat, ignoring the heat flushing her cheeks. She didn't want to be attracted to a man she didn't respect.

Focusing, she snapped on a glove and pulled the letter from the bag. She read aloud, "Drop the de Lugo case, Judge, or you'll be sorry. You've already lost a sister and a wife. What would those kids do if they lost you, too? You're not safe anywhere. Your home, your office, your gym, your bed—there's nowhere we can't get to you. If you don't drop the case, you'd better update your will."

Carly passed the letter to Mason and looked up at the handsome judge. "The de Lugo trial." A statement, not a question. She knew about the trial.

"Yes, the trial of Ricardo de Lugo and his murdering band of cohorts is set to start in less than one week. Six days to be exact. Two years of undercover work by two FBI agents finally netted enough evidence to put him away for life—possibly even give him the death penalty." He paused. "Assuming we make it to trial. No matter how much protection is offered, it seems this man has eyes and ears everywhere." He gestured to the letter. "Someone who knows me pretty well seems to be passing on information."

Carly shifted. "We have marshals on the FBI agents' families, too. As for this—" she waved the letter "—he doesn't necessarily have to know you well. A little research online probably told him everything ever published in the newspaper about you. But," she mused, "whoever wrote this appears to be educated. Proper grammar, flawless punctuation…"

Seth stood. "I've got to get back to my partner. I left him guarding a prisoner who gets on your nerves after five minutes in his company. He'll be ready for a break."

Mason shook his hand. "We've got this covered. Thanks for your help."

"Anytime." Seth left, and Mason turned to Nicholas. "You're still determined to go out there?"

A hard sheen flattened his gold-green eyes. "Absolutely."

"When will your current trial wrap up?"

"I'm hoping by this afternoon. It's a pretty straightforward case."

"After that, what would you think about hiding out in a safe house until the de Lugo trial starts?"

He didn't answer at first. "If it were just threats against me, I would say forget it. I've had training. But the kids..." He stood. "I've got to change my shirt and get into my robe. Let me think about it."

"There's really nothing to think about, sir. All the training in the world won't stop a sniper's bullet. And while we can't exactly stop it, either, we give you a better chance of ducking when one heads your way. You need us, whether you like it or not."

Carly watched Nick and Mason square off.

"Think of the children, Nicholas," Carly offered softly. When she'd first met him two years ago, he hadn't had the children. His wife and sister had been alive. She'd seen pictures of the kids, and he'd told her about them in detail, like the doting uncle he was.

Since then a lot had happened. He'd lost two women he'd loved, gained two children—and released a killer to kill again.

She blinked that last thought away.

He blew out a breath and undid the buttons on his cuffs. Forearms roped with strength emerged as he shoved the sleeves up to his elbows; Carly swallowed hard, desperately trying to convince herself she was *not* feeling another tug of attraction.

What was wrong with her?

"Look," Nick said as he headed for the door, "we just moved here to Spartanburg a year ago. My mother moved out to California to take care of my sick aunt, and my latest nanny up and quit on me so I have a friend filling in." He shook his head. "Since my sister died in the car wreck with my wife, there's been no real consistency in my niece and nephew's lives. Lindsey and Christopher need that. They crave that. My house is about as safe as you can get. Granted, it's not hard to find, but I'm not listed in the phone book, either. As for the information online, that was all newspaper stuff. Nothing about where I live." He shot Carly and Mason a hard look. "If I let you move in to my house, can you keep the kids safe while they go through their usual daily routine?"

Carly glanced at Mason, who shrugged. To Nick, she said, "Yes. The children weren't threatened. That's a good thing. But it's obvious the de Lugos are trying to hit you where you're vulnerable. They mention the kids, but there's no overt threat to them. However, if you ask me, that's still a threat, no matter how subtle. We'll take extra precautions with the children, of course, but your safety is our main concern right now, since you were the one threatened."

She wondered if she would believe those words one day, but they seemed to ease Nick's mind a little. For her, though, just the fact that there were children involved would keep her up nights until this assignment came to an end.

Nick nodded. "Then pack your bags. I'll tell my house-keeper you guys are moving in for a while."

Carly watched Nicholas walk up the steps and settle himself into the judge's chair. The bailiff took up residence off to the side. As the jury filed in, she noted their serious expressions. Several looked at the door through which the defendant would enter. Others watched their feet, never lifting their eyes from the floor even as they settled into their chairs.

Interesting and odd, she noted, picking up on the undercurrents flowing around the group.

The prosecutor already sat at his table.

The door opened, and Seth and his partner led an orange-suited, leg-shackled prisoner through it.

Harrison Frasier. On trial for the murder of a local stockbroker. He claimed he was innocent, but the security video captured him in the office at the time of the murder even though it didn't actually show him pulling the trigger. The murder weapon was never found. However, a witness and DNA, along with the video, almost assured a guilty verdict.

Harrison Frasier. Carly tapped her lip as she studied the man. Good-looking, athletic build, early twenties. Looked like the boy next door you'd hire to mow your grass.

The jury foreman rose. Judge Floyd nodded to the man. "Has the jury reached a verdict, sir?"

"We have, Your Honor." He carried it to the bench and handed it over.

Nicholas read it and handed it back without blinking an eye or changing expression, although Carly wondered if she was the only one who noticed the muscle jumping along his jawline.

The foreman returned to his chair and stood in front of it.

Harrison Frasier stood.

Nicholas cleared his throat and asked, "Would you please read the verdict?"

"We, the jury, find the defendant not guilty on all charges."

Pandemonium broke loose.

"No!" A woman in her forties stood, tears streaming

down her cheeks. Carly recognized her from the news. She was the wife of the victim. An older gentleman who looked to be her father wrapped an arm around her shoulder and simply stared at Nicholas, then at the foreman.

Carly had to strain to hear the man's words over the chaos. "How could you let this happen?"

Nicholas stood and headed down the steps.

"Why didn't you do something, Judge? You should have done something." This time she heard the man loud and clear.

Nick stopped and looked out at the man who'd hollered. Sadness covered his features, and he shook his head.

"You'll pay for this!"

Carly's attention meter stood at full alert as she and Mason hurried to Nick's side. A threat? She glanced at the officer nearest the door. He had his eyes on the individual who'd issued the threat. Carly relaxed a tad as she realized the man had directed his last comment to the defendant, who now stood a free man. Harrison Frasier laughed and turned his back on the elderly man.

Eyes blazing, cheeks still wet, the victim's wife grabbed her father's hand and pulled him toward the double rear doors of the courtroom, pushing her way through the throng of reporters and flashing cameras.

At Nicholas's side, Carly looked at Harrison and saw him hug his lawyer and another young woman. A sister? A wife? Girlfriend?

Escorting the judge back to his chambers adjacent to the courtroom, Carly opened the door. Mason entered, weapon drawn.

Nicholas stood just inside the door next to Carly. "Come on. Isn't this a bit extreme?"

She just looked at him, trying not to admire his handsome features. Right now, they were hard, as though chiseled in stone. The only imperfection was on his jawline where he'd sliced himself with the razor.

Distracting herself from that line of thought, she asked, "Haven't you heard, 'Better safe than sorry'?"

She thought she heard his teeth click together but was glad when he said nothing else. She really didn't want to argue with him. Mason came out of the bathroom. "All clear."

Carly heard the rasp of the zipper on Nicholas' robe. He tossed it over the back of the chair. "Let's get out of here. I want to check on my family."

Gladly.

Carly led the way out the door, checking the hallway as she listened to his footfalls behind her. She shivered as she felt his gaze touch her back. What was he thinking? Was he wondering what she thought of him? That it was because of him that her friend and mentor had been killed? Did he even know?

Mason brought up the rear as they approached the back door of the building. Shoving ahead of Carly and Nicholas, he pushed open the door. Carly laid a restraining hand on Nicholas. "Wait a minute."

An impatient sigh hissed from him, but he held his tongue and stood still.

Mason's head popped back in. "We're clear."

Carly stepped out, looked both ways then motioned for Nicholas to follow. "Give Mason your keys. He'll drive your car."

"That's not necessary. I'll be…"

"Hey, Judge!"

The trio turned as one to see Harrison Frasier reveling in his newly declared freedom. One hand on the passenger door of a minivan, the man offered Nicholas a salute with his free hand. "Great job in there, my friend."

"I'm not your friend, you—"

A loud pop cut off Nicholas's outraged growl.

Carly reacted by giving Nicholas a hard shove behind the nearest parked car and throwing herself on top of him. If a bullet was headed his way, it was going through her first. But when she looked back, it was Harrison who lay on the ground, a dark red stain growing across his chest.

TWO

"Get inside," she ordered as she scrambled into a crouched position beside him, "just in case our shooter is still somewhere nearby."

Without comment, pulse pounding with adrenaline, Nicholas pulled himself to his feet and pushed the door open for Carly, then followed her through it. Mason headed over to the scene.

Nicholas's brain processed Carly's words as he leaned against the wall to catch his breath. His heart pounded in his chest as his mind replayed the image of Harrison being hit with the bullet.

Shock quickly followed the surprise on the man's arrogant features. Then he'd almost looked pleading as he'd dropped to the ground.

Absently, Nicholas heard Carly talking to someone on her radio. Calling for help? His mind went to Lindsey and Christopher. He glanced at his watch. They'd be home from school by now, and he had to make sure they were safe. Carly had assured him they weren't in any danger, but he wanted to hear that for himself from someone who had eyes on them.

Even as he subconsciously waited for the sound of

another bullet, he yanked out his cell phone and pressed the speed-dial number.

"Hello?"

Forcing a calmness into his voice he didn't feel, he asked, "Debbie, is everything all right at the house?"

"Hi, Nick. Everything's fine. Two U.S. Marshals showed up at the children's school saying you'd been threatened and they were just there to keep an eye on things. They followed me home and are still here. Are you okay?"

He closed his eyes, picturing the children's nanny. Debbie had been a blessing in one of his greatest times of need. When his mother had decided to leave for California, the daughter of his best friend and fellow judge, Wayne Thomas, had volunteered to fill in as caretaker for Lindsey and Christopher until he could find someone on a permanent basis. "Yes, I'm fine." He'd tell her about the shooting later. "I'm just going to be a bit delayed in getting home, all right?"

"Sure, Nick. No problem."

"Thanks, Deb." The fact that he'd been threatened wouldn't freak her out, but she'd be on high alert. Her father, Wayne Thomas, was also a judge, so she knew about threats and protective details. However, the fact that Nicholas had been present when a shooter actually killed someone might be a bit much for her.

He hung up and watched Carly walk toward him, holstering her weapon. His heart flipped into a weird beat at the sight of her, face flushed, dark curls escaping her ponytail. Mirrored sunglasses covered her eyes, so he couldn't read her expression. He swallowed hard. Was he attracted to her? Surely not. He had appreciated her friendship two years ago. But he'd been a married man then—and no matter how troubled his marriage had been, he would never have jeopardized it by allowing himself to get close to another woman. Still, Carly had been easy to talk to, a true friend.

Focusing on her words, he pushed his thoughts away. "The shooter got away."

Nicholas narrowed his eyes and determined to pull his own gun from the wall safe just as soon as he got home. The door opened behind him as he questioned Carly. "Why Harrison Frasier?"

"I have no idea."

"I do."

Nicholas turned to see Mason step inside.

A quick glimpse behind Mason as the door shut showed authorities swarming the area. The press had arrived in record time, since they were already on the premises for the trial.

Harrison had already been transported from the scene. Yellow tape marked the area where the crime-scene unit now worked. The door clicked shut, and the deputy marshal held something in his left hand that he offered to Carly. She took it.

"What is it?" Nick asked.

"Apparently, our guy is fond of letters. Two in one day."

"So, the shooter isn't the father of the victim." Nick stated the thought that had been in his head ever since he'd seen Harrison go down.

"No, I'm going to say not."

Nicholas leaned over Carly's shoulder to read. Her scent swirled around him and, against his better judgment, he breathed in deep. Then the typed words pulled the air from his lungs.

"Do you understand our power now, Judge Nicholas Floyd?" he read aloud. "Mr. Frasier was guilty. You know it and we know it. But we wanted a not-guilty verdict. So we got it. Drop the de Lugo case or you will die and leave poor Lindsey and Christopher true orphans."

His back teeth ground against each other. Through tight lips, he muttered, "I knew someone got to that jury as soon as I saw the verdict."

"What do you mean?" Carly asked.

"The evidence was too clear-cut—and Harrison was too cocky. It should have been an open-and-shut case. The de Lugos got to the jury and swayed the judgment—just to prove to me they could."

"How many jurors do you think they got to?" Mason asked.

He shrugged. "It would only take one if he or she had the right personality. But I'm guessing it was probably more than one. All you have to find is a juror with a kid. Threaten the kid, and get the juror to do anything you want."

"Then we need to talk to the jurors," Carly stated.

He shot her a wry look. "If you think it would do any good. We already know who was doing the threatening, but yeah, we'll send a report in and let the proper authorities take care of it." His jaw hardened. "Can't hurt to have one more charge to bring against the de Lugos."

"All right, we need to get you into a secured area." Mason shoved his gun in his shoulder holster. "Right now, that's going to be your home. How many people live there?"

"There's six of us right now. My housekeeper, Stella, and her husband, Carl, a nanny, Debbie, myself and the children."

"Two marshals will stay on the children as they go to and from school. You might want to consider letting the nanny go for her own safety."

"Fine. What about Stella? She's trained to defend herself."

Carly remembered the woman from the last time she'd been in his home. "She's an ex-police officer. Her husband is the groundskeeper, right?"

"Right. She's the niece of my mother's best friend. She was wounded in the line of duty and took an early retirement. By the time she'd recovered, Mom decided she couldn't handle the housework anymore and asked Stella if she'd be interested in doing it. She wanted someone she knew and trusted and didn't want to go to all the trouble of interviews, etcetera. I didn't think Stella'd be interested, but fortunately for us, she jumped on it. She said she needed something to keep her busy, but I think she enjoyed being around us and the children since she couldn't have any of her own. She and her husband, Carl, live in the mother-in-law suite attached to the house. To ask them to leave would really put them out."

"They can stay as long as they understand the dangers."

Nicholas rubbed his eyes. "I'll give them the option of moving into a hotel at my expense, although I don't know what they would do with their two dogs."

Mason raised a brow. "Dogs are good. They bark."

"True. In this new house, I had the security system upgraded with motion sensors and security cameras. Plus, I had a wrought-iron fence installed. And all of this in a gated community."

"What else?" Carly urged.

"It's an electric fence. If anyone tries to go over it, they'll get a pretty nasty shock. That's about it."

"It's better than a lot we've worked with in the past." Thank goodness. The thought of Nicholas or one of the children ending up dead sent shivers of fear all over her. The thought of being around Nick 24/7 made her stomach clench, too, although she wasn't sure if it was from dread or the pull of attraction she couldn't deny feeling.

She shrugged off her feelings. Time to do her job. "All right, let's get going." Carly held up the paper bag with the second letter. "I'm just going to turn this over to the crime-scene guys. Then we can get out of here."

Two minutes later, they were on the road. Carly drove the unmarked police car and Mason followed behind in Nicholas's car. He watched Carly's slender fingers grip the wheel.

When she'd invaded his home two years ago, just a few months before his wife's death, they'd butted heads on the protection issue yet Carly in his home brought a certain peace to the household that had been distinctly absent before her arrival.

His wife, Miriam, had basically closed herself in their bedroom and become a hermit for the duration of Carly and her partner's stay. It had been a relief, he remembered with guilt. Miriam had changed in their six years of marriage, depression stealing her sweet, happy-go-lucky personality away from him.

She'd wanted a baby, and they hadn't been able to have one. The fact that no doctor could tell them why just compounded the problem. His home life had started to unravel and quickly became unbearable. And while Nick never thought he would consider divorce, he had to admit it had crossed his mind in the weeks before Miriam had been killed.

Then the marshals had arrived. He smiled at the irony. He hadn't wanted the marshals at that point in time any more than he wanted them this time.

But then he thought about the nights they'd sat up talking, the three of them; Carly, Mason and himself. A friendship had formed. Since then, he and Mason had gotten together for the occasional game of racquetball or met up at the high school football stadium to watch the local teams go at it.

He hadn't seen Carly since they'd found out the threats had been a hoax. But that hadn't kept him from keeping up with her.

Through Mason, and frequent chats with Ian, Carly's brother and Nick's former college roommate, Nick had gotten snatches of what her life had been like over the last two years.

He also knew that she blamed him for something he'd had no control over. He'd let a killer go. The one who'd ended up murdering Hank, a good friend of hers. His stomach twisted itself in knots every time he thought about it. He didn't have to wonder what she thought of him.

He could read the wariness in her eyes. The borderline contempt she tried to hide.

And yet, because he knew the kind of person she was, he had no doubt she would do her job to the death for him if it came to it.

He vowed it wouldn't.

Lord, let me get a chance to explain why I had to let that man go. Please. And let her understand.

"Why did you move from the house at the beach?"

Her question seemed to come out of left field as he shook off his thoughts. "Because we all needed a change." He pictured the large, sprawling estate and felt a pang of nostalgia. "I loved that house, but I built it for my wife. When she and my sister were killed..." He shrugged and sighed. "Plus the children had to ride past the accident site every day on their way to school."

"How did they even know where it happened?"

"Lindsey was having nightmares about it. The therapist suggested taking her to the site and placing a memorial there. We built a little cross and put her mother's name on it, and I let her pound it into the ground. She seemed to get a little better almost overnight."

"But?"

"As time passed, it continued to affect them. Especially Lindsey. She'd do better, then worse, constantly back and forth. If there'd been another route to the school, I would have taken it, but there wasn't. I suggested changing schools, and Lindsey completely freaked at the idea, so..." He shrugged again. "Then Mom left for California..." A deep breath. "When my buddy Wayne encouraged me to come back to Spartanburg so we'd have some support, it seemed like the right thing to do. With my sister gone, I became an only child and didn't have any close family around, so we moved." He turned the tables on her. "Why do you do this?"

She shot him a startled look. "What? My job?"

"Yes."

She blinked then focused back on the road. "Because I like it."

"I know a lot of your family is in law enforcement. But why did *you* choose it?"

A faint smile curved her lips, and he wondered what they'd feel like. The thought came out of nowhere, and he quickly put on the mental brakes.

Someone was threatening him.

It was Carly's job to protect him.

End of story.

"I don't know. I never had any major catastrophe in my life or anything that pushed me toward this kind of career. But I grew up with it. It's what I know. I suppose it was a natural choice with Ian being in the army and my dad being a cop. He was just so *satisfied* every time he put a bad guy in jail. It was literally the highlight of his day. That really influenced me." She smiled at him. "He retired a couple of years ago."

"Ah, so that's why."

She shrugged. "It probably had a lot to do with it. But I just really like the job."

"Then why don't you want to do it?"

Carly nearly swerved off the road. Instead, she took a moment to gather her composure and said, "Why would you say that?"

"I get the feeling that you don't want to be here. With me."

She bit her lip. How to explain? Should she even bother explaining? And how had he picked up on that, anyway? Had she gotten that bad at hiding her feelings?

But he was trained to read people. And he'd read her like a first-grade primer.

Squaring her jaw, she shot him a look. "Your feelings are wrong." Sort of. Actually, they were dead-on. "I want to do my job. I *will* do my job, no matter what it takes, got it?"

He remained silent for a moment, his eyes searching for things she'd rather keep hidden. "Do your feelings have anything to do with the fact that I let Richie Hardin go and he killed your friend Hank?"

Bingo.

She blinked and did her best to cover her initial impulse to blurt out "yes!" Instead, she took a deep breath and said in a low voice. "That's irrelevant to what I have to do here with you. I don't want to talk about Hank's death or the cause of it."

"Sooner or later, we're going to have to, I think."

"I don't know why. It has nothing to do with my ability

to do my job. I'll do mine, you do yours. Put the bad guys away instead of letting them walk, and everyone wins."

"Carly..." He sighed, and she saw him struggle with whatever it was he wanted to say. "Fine. But we *will* discuss it. Soon. Just don't let your negative feelings for me or my judicial decisions put my family in danger."

His words sent a shaft of pain through her. Did he really think she would be that unprofessional and allow that to happen? For a moment, she couldn't speak. She just pulled into the gated drive and waited for Mason to pull in behind her in Nicholas's car and use the remote to open the gate.

Soon the iron gates began their inward swing. Carly stepped on the gas and wound her way up the drive to the front of the house and parked behind the brown sedan that belonged to the two marshals inside. Instead of opening her door, she swallowed hard and turned to look at Nicholas.

He unhooked his seat belt and caught her gaze. When she was certain she had his full attention, she said, "I'm a professional. I'll do my job regardless of my feelings. If it comes down to it, I'll die for you or those children. Are we clear?"

He lifted a brow, then gave a slow nod. "Crystal. In fact, now you've got me a little worried. I don't want you to die for me, Carly."

She gave him a tight smile. "I don't want to, either. But I will if it comes down to it. That's all you have to know."

End of discussion.

Carly climbed from the car and swept the grounds with a practiced eye. Everything seemed quiet. She drew in a deep breath of air and got her bearings. She could do this. It's what she'd trained for, lived for...and would someday probably die for.

But right now, Nicholas and the children were counting on her.

Then the front door opened and two marshals stepped outside. She recognized them as a team she'd worked with on a number of occasions. "Grady. Maria."

Mason shook hands with them. Grady, a tall, trim man with salt-and-pepper hair, spoke. "Everything's quiet. One of us has done a perimeter sweep every fifteen minutes. The dogs have been calm, and nothing has set off any alarms."

Carly motioned for Nicholas to go into the house, worried about him standing out in the open. She might have a problem respecting him, but she sure didn't want him dead.

He nodded and moved to stand inside the doorway, off to the left. Out of sight of anyone watching the house, but not out of earshot. She knew he wanted to hear every word the four marshals might exchange.

Maria came from a long line of cops. Stocky and short, she was light on her feet in spite of her build. Maria was good at her job and didn't let anything get in the way of her goal: to keep her assignment alive.

"The kids are good kids," Maria said. "Better watch that girl, though. I have a feeling she might be a handful. We'll be back tomorrow. Let us know if you need anything before then."

"Will do. Thanks."

Carly and Mason said their goodbyes to Grady and Maria and followed Nicholas farther into the house. She shut the door and glanced around.

Nice.

Not extravagant, but definitely upper middle class. She'd done her homework on the man but remembered her brother Ian telling her that Nicholas had designed a video game that made him a lot of money before he'd even graduated college.

He probably could have gone into the gaming business and become a multimillionaire, but his passion was the law. And he'd succeeded there, too.

For the most part.

When he wasn't letting violent criminals out to kill good cops. Hank and Lily, two people who'd become good friends. Hank who had taught her everything she knew. And now he was dead, and Lily a grieving widow. Her gut tightened at the thought, and she pulled in a deep breath. *Don't go there, Carly, or you'll go crazy. Keep your objectivity. Remember, you don't know the whole story.*

But she knew enough. Enough to know she'd better keep her guard up and her emotions under control when it came to Nicholas Floyd.

"Debbie? You in here?" Nick called as he walked into the den area.

"I'm right here, Nick."

Carly turned at the intrusion of the feminine voice. A pretty young woman in her late twenties stood at the entrance to the kitchen, wiping her hands on a dish towel. She had her reddish-brown hair pulled up in an attractive loose ponytail. She stopped when she saw Carly and Mason. "Oh, sorry, I didn't realize we were having more company."

"These are two more U.S. Marshals, Deb." His dark gaze swept back to Carly. "This is Debbie Thomas, the children's nanny."

"For now." Debbie flashed a smile and held out a hand that Carly and Mason took turns shaking. "I'm filling in until Nick finds a permanent one." She flushed and said, "I have to confess I was just popping some popcorn for the kids. I know it's close to dinnertime, but…"

Carly just noticed the mouthwatering smell of freshly popped popcorn. It reminded her she hadn't eaten dinner yet.

Nicholas gave a small smile, a mere twitch of his lips, then said, "That's fine, Debbie. A little popcorn before dinner won't hurt them." The he blew out a rough sigh. "Since Mom left to take care of her sister in California, I haven't had the time or energy to look for someone to…" He shot the young woman an apologetic look.

Debbie patted the man's arm. "It's all right, Nick."

Watching the interchange, Carly couldn't help but wonder if there was something more between the two than a business arrangement. The little twinge of jealousy took her by surprise.

Oh, no, there was no way she was jealous. She wasn't remotely interested in starting any kind of relationship, especially not with an assignment. Period.

Kicking those feelings as far to the curb as she could get them, she pulled out her notebook. "All right, let's go over some ground rules, shall we?"

"Are they the same rules as last time?" he asked.

She couldn't help the small smile that curved the right side of her lips. "Yes, pretty much."

"Then I think I'm covered."

Mason stepped forward. "Where are the kids?"

Debbie answered, "In the playroom upstairs. They're watching a movie."

"Hence the popcorn." Nicholas scrubbed a hand over his face and waved them all into the den area. "Have a seat. Deb, you take the popcorn up to the kids, and I'll fill you in on anything you need to know in a little bit. We'll have dinner in about an hour, all right?"

Consternation flashed briefly in her pretty eyes. Then she shrugged. "Fine. Mrs. Jefferson left a roast with vegetables cooking in the Crock-pot. There's plenty to feed everyone." She sent a smile in Mason and Carly's direction. "Nice meeting you." Then she was gone, whirling away in a scented cloud of popcorn and some fruity perfume that made Carly's nose itch.

Mason looked at Carly. "I know Maria and Grady checked out the house, the windows and everything, but I'd feel better giving it a once-over myself. I'll be right back."

She nodded, and Mason headed up the stairs.

The duo left behind sat on the couch, and Carly looked at Nicholas. "Is there any way you would consider recusing yourself from this trial?"

"Absolutely not. I refuse to give in to scare tactics, threats, whatever. I don't operate that way."

Carly wasn't surprised by his answer. "Then we're going to have to figure out the best way to keep everyone safe until this trial is over."

THREE

While Mason secured the house, Carly watched the interactions of Nicholas and his niece and nephew. Lindsey, twelve, stood almost as tall as Carly. The quiet girl was reed thin, with blue eyes that saw everything.

She hadn't been nearly as welcoming as her seven-year-old brother, Christopher, who'd given her a high five and invited her to his room to see his fish. "I gotta have fish," he explained. "I'm 'lergic to cats, and I can't play with the dogs. I have asthma, too. The fish don't bother my lungs."

Asthma. She made a mental note of the fact.

"I thought you guys were watching a movie and stuffing yourselves on popcorn so you could sit down at dinner and say you're not hungry," Nick teased.

Christopher gave a belly laugh. Lindsey had the art of eye rolling down perfect, and she seemed to feel the need to display it at every opportunity.

Five minutes after meeting Lindsey, Carly discovered her outlook on life consisted of a combination of waiting-for-the-other-shoe-to-drop and roll-your-eyes-at-anything-an-adult-says attitude.

To make things easier on Carly and Mason, the Jeffersons had moved into the main house with their two dogs.

They'd declined the hotel room. The second-floor guest room was a compromise.

Debbie moved into the room at the end of the hall. She seemed to take everything in stride. "I've been in this situation before with Dad." A hand batted at the air. "It's usually no big deal. He's gotten threats before, and nothing happened. So I'm not leaving when the children need me. That would just be one more inconsistency in their lives. And we have protection, right?"

Carly stared at her. "Are you sure? This could be a tense few days before the trial starts." Even the fact that a man had been murdered as a message to her boss only caused a minor hesitation in the young woman.

She bit her lip, eyes darting between Carly and Mason, then back to Nicholas. Her jaw firmed. "No, I'm staying."

"Great, more people in this house." Lindsey rolled her eyes.

Nick shot her a look. "Watch it, Linds."

The girl clenched her jaw and stomped toward the stairs.

Debbie frowned and went after her.

Christopher slipped a small hand into Carly's and looked up at her with a gap-toothed grin. "I'm glad you're here."

She patted his head and knelt down on his level to grin back at him. "I'm glad I'm here, too." She stood then looked at Nicholas. "It's my turn to check the grounds."

"Come on, kiddo." He motioned for his nephew to transfer his hand from Carly's to his. "Let's go see if dinner's going to be ready soon. I'm starving."

After a quiet and tense meal, Debbie retired to her room at the end of the hall. Nick saw the children off to bed, and Carly walked the perimeter of the house one more time, her nerves stretched taut. Right now, she could relate to Lindsey's waiting-for-the-other-shoe-to-drop mentality.

It was too quiet. Yet the silence seemed loud. Filled with expectation, anticipation—waiting.

But for what?

Nothing good, that was for sure.

She shivered even as sweat broke out across her forehead.

The darkness pressed in, although the floodlights illuminated her path. The night smelled of dogwood and honeysuckle. She walked the darkened edge, not wanting to make herself a target should anyone be watching from beyond the fence.

The two dogs, she'd learned, were retired police K-9s the Jeffersons had adopted after Stella Jefferson's departure from the force. Carly had made friends with them, then turned them loose.

Pushing the earpiece deeper into her ear, she said, "All's clear out here."

"We're settled in here," Mason's voice came back to her. "You want first watch?"

"Sure. What about the kids? Do they seem all right?"

"Yeah. Well, Christopher and I are big buds now. The girl…um…not so much."

"I noticed that, too. They've had so much upheaval in their young lives…"

"I know. Just FYI, our judge is armed."

She stopped just on the edge of the light, her eyes scanning the darkness even as her brain processed the conversation. "Excuse me?"

"He got his gun from a safe and loaded it."

Carly thought about that for a minute then said slowly, "Well, he's had the training. He knows how to use it."

"Yeah, that was my take on it."

"Then, good. I think."

The floodlights clicked off. Her heart kicked up a notch as she froze. "Mason, did you do that?"

A quiet beat stretched between them. Then he said in a low voice. "No. The lights went off in here, too. Call for help and get in here."

The other shoe had just dropped—with a bang.

Nick had just pointedly told Lindsey to get ready for bed. "And could you please lose the attitude? They're here to help us." He wouldn't admit he wished he could throw a temper tantrum himself about the whole situation. But that wasn't going to help anything.

Another eye roll. "Right."

Frustration bit at him. Ever since her mother and aunt had been killed, Lindsey's personality had done a one-eighty. She used to be so sweet, laughing at his silly attempts to bring a smile to her face, offering hugs with guileless spontaneity.

Then her mother and aunt died, and the bottom had dropped out of her world. Her grandmother leaving hadn't helped the situation, either. Nick understood why his mom felt she had to leave. There simply wasn't anyone else to take care of his aunt. But tell that to Lindsey.

With a sigh, he studied his niece's mutinous expression and supposed she was coping the only way she knew how.

Then the lights went out.

Frustration morphed into concern, then outright fear as he realized what was happening.

"Lindsey, get over here." He pressed the button on his iPhone to illuminate the room. The glow caught her startled, fearful expression.

"Why?" she demanded.

He strode to her and grasped her wrist in a light grip. "The power just went out, and I don't know why yet. Stay with me and head to Christopher's room."

"I've got him." Carly's voiced reached out to him a few moments later in the dark. "Everyone stay together while we get to the safe area."

An area she could defend, he thought. Drawing in a calming breath, he said, "The laundry room would be best. No windows and only one way in."

"Good job. I'd already picked that place myself. We don't have much time. The alarm wasn't tripped, and without power it won't be."

"Yes, it will. I have a generator that kicks in for the alarm system. And the laundry room is off the kitchen."

"You and the kids get in there."

"Get my dog, Uncle Nick," Christopher cried suddenly. "Pepper. I don't want the bad people to get him!"

Carly shot him a look. "Dog?"

"A stuffed animal he sleeps with." He placed a hand on Christopher's head. "He's safe and sound, tucked under your bed last time I saw him, okay?" Then he looked at Carly. "What about Debbie and the Jeffersons?" No way was he going to tuck his tail and run when people he cared about were in danger.

"Mason has them." She spoke into her radio. "Meet us in the kitchen." To Nicholas, she said, "Follow me and stay away from the windows."

As they descended the slightly curved staircase, the sound of barking reached his ears. "The dogs aren't happy. Someone's on the grounds."

"Or somewhere around the fence. I wish you had some closer neighbors who'd check out all the racket."

The barking escalated.

A shadow passed the bay window in the den. "They're

outside the house," he whispered. Lindsey clutched his hand, the sullen preteen now a scared young girl. Both children remained silent, eyes wide, breaths rasping. She noted Christopher seemed to be wheezing a little. "Do you have his inhaler?"

"In my pocket." Nicholas fumbled in the front pocket of his jeans.

His heart thudded, not so much in fear for himself as for the kids and his staff. And the marshals. Most specifically, Carly.

God, please don't let anyone get hurt. I know she's skilled in her job, but I can't live with someone else I know dying…

Her right hand gripped Christopher's; her left curled around the gun. She motioned them left at the bottom of the steps, across the den and into the kitchen. She opened the laundry-room door and said, "All right. In you go. Lock it behind you."

Thankfully, he'd installed the lock on the laundry-room door when the kids had come to live with him. He hadn't wanted Christopher to accidentally get into the household supplies he kept in there.

Although if someone was determined to get in, neither the door nor the lock would hold against a swift kick with a booted foot.

Nick felt the weight of his weapon pressing against his lower back and itched to pull it out. Why hadn't the alarm gone off? Then he realized that he hadn't heard the generator kick in.

Lips pressed into a thin line, he motioned the kids in. Mason, Debbie and the Jeffersons appeared next to him. He reached across the counter and grabbed the telephone.

Dead.

Grimly, he reported, "No power and no generator for some reason. Phone line's been cut, too."

"Great," Mason muttered.

"Get in," Nick urged. Debbie led the way. The children immediately attached themselves to her side. Nick handed the inhaler to her, and she passed it to Christopher, who stuck it in his mouth for a good puff. His eyes pleaded with Nick as he whined, "I want Pepper."

Nick rubbed his head. "I'll go get him in just a minute, okay?"

"Promise?"

"Promise. You just concentrate on breathing, okay?"

Christopher gave a reluctant nod. The Jeffersons entered the room, and Nicholas shut the door.

Carly looked at him. "What are you doing? Get in there."

He narrowed his eyes on her and pulled his gun from the back of his waistband. "Not a chance."

"This is what *we're* here for, remember?" she protested.

Mason motioned toward the front of the house. "No time to argue. Judge, you stay back and out of sight if you can. Use the gun if necessary."

"You're not making this any easier." Carly's nose flared as she shot him a look mixed with anger and fear. Nicholas understood her anger, wondered at her fear.

"This is my fight," he insisted. "I won't deny I might need help, but I refuse to sit on the sidelines while somebody else fights it."

Carly bit her lip and forced aside visions of him lying in a pool of blood.

Her gut clenched and a protest hovered on her lips. Then a loud crash came from just ahead. Carly stepped in front of Nicholas and pointed her gun in the direction of the sound. "Freeze!"

Running footsteps sounded. The flash of a large shadow darted around a corner. Nicholas brushed past her and took off in pursuit. Mason ran the other way, and Carly knew he was looking to cut off the intruder.

She counted one person inside the house.

But how many were outside?

Sirens sounded in the distance. Help was on the way. She hoped the approaching authorities would scare off whoever was on the property. The dogs were barking like crazy. How had the intruders gotten past them?

Carly followed Nicholas, determined to back up whatever he was doing. She'd hold on to the tongue-lashing she wanted to give him until after everyone was safe.

Rounding the corner, she pulled up short. Nicholas had his back up against the side of the house, his gun held steady, aiming into the dark. "What is it?"

"Two of them ran toward the woods."

Carly radioed it in. A police helicopter would head their way. They'd also notify the authorities to be on the lookout for cars coming from this direction.

"Carly!"

Mason. She motioned for Nicholas to follow her back into the house. Police now swarmed the property. Mason stood in the den area talking to several officers and barking out orders.

"What is it, Mason?"

Her partner looked up as she walked in. "He—or they—got away, but one of the dogs snagged this."

With a gloved hand, he held up a piece of fabric. Carly wrinkled her nose. "What is it?"

"A piece of a shirt, I think." In his other latex-covered hand, he held up wire cutters. "We'll have the lab test this for prints, but I don't think they'll get anything. Whoever is after Nick is smart and they'd have had gloves on. It's a no-brainer."

"Still, we've got to try. We might get pleasantly surprised and catch a break."

Mason grunted his disagreement as he set the two pieces of evidence aside to be taken to the lab, but didn't argue. She knew he secretly hoped she was right.

Nicholas ran his fingers through his already tousled hair and sighed. "Why didn't the generator kick in when they cut the power? And how did they get past the dogs?"

"The dogs were maced," Mason informed them. "They came prepared to take the dogs out. As for the generator, I checked on that. It's been dismantled." Mason paced from one end of the den back to them.

"How?" Nicholas snapped. "It's in a closed area that blends in with the house. How would they know where to find it?"

Carly drew in a deep breath and shared a glance with Mason, who said, "Our intruders did their homework. They've probably been doing it ever since they found out you were going to be sitting on the case. These guys are good, professional killers." He sighed and rubbed his chin. "But why strike here? Professional killers prefer to work from a distance. Why didn't they shoot you instead of Harrison Frasier?"

Carly sighed. "Good point. Unless," she pondered, "they don't really care if you're dead or not. They just want you off the case. If they can scare you off, why bother to kill you?" She threw her hands into the air. "Who knows? I do know this—we've got our work cut out for us."

Nicholas shot her a ferocious frown. A hand reached up to rub the back of his neck, and Carly's palms actually itched with the sudden impulse to massage the tension from his shoulders.

Get a grip, she ordered herself and curled her traitorous hands into fists. She stepped forward and placed a hand on Nicholas's arm almost before she thought about what she was doing.

Footsteps sounded and Carly jumped back, but not before Nick's frown softened and his eyes glinted with something she wasn't able to put a label on.

Lindsey rushed into the room and wrapped her arms around her uncle's waist. Christopher grabbed a leg and held on. His breathing seemed much better, Carly noticed.

Nicholas placed a hand on each of the children's shoulders and reassured them with pats and hugs. "Everything's fine, kids. Go on up and get in your beds. I know it's going to be almost impossible to sleep, but you try for now." He shot a pleading look at Debbie. "I know you're not on duty at night, but do you think…"

"I'll take care of them." Debbie stepped forward and held out her hands. "Come on, Chris, let's go make sure Pepper's all right and give him a big hug." Christopher eyes brightened, but he still gave one last lingering glance at his uncle before following Debbie to the stairs. "Can I jump on the bed, Debbie?"

The woman gave a low chuckle. "Maybe just a few bounces."

Lindsey seemed to have found her attitude again and glared at him. "Why don't you just drop the stupid case so we can have our lives back?"

With that parting shot, she turned on her heel, shoving past Debbie and Christopher.

"Lindsey…" Nick's voice trailed off when he realized his niece had no intention of heeding his call. With a sigh, he shut his eyes and stood without moving for several seconds.

Carly knew he was wondering if he should go after her or not, and her heart ached for him.

She offered him her unsolicited advice, keeping her voice low and trying to offer encouragement. "Give her some space. She'll be all right."

Although why she wanted to make him feel better was beyond her. How many hours had she lain awake thinking about her mentor, Hank, who had been cut down coming out of his granddaughter's ballet recital? How many times had she railed at the heavens for placing a judge on the bench who didn't care that he was releasing a monster back into the world?

And yet…she felt something for him. Her traitorous heart kept wondering if maybe she had things skewed. Maybe she didn't know all the facts about that case.

"I know," Nick finally said. "She's just had it so rough for so long—and now this."

A loud thump sounded from upstairs, and Carly started, her hand on her gun. Mason took up guard next to Nick.

"It's just Christopher," Nick said, holding up a hand to stop her progress.

She paused. "What do you mean?"

A guilty flush started appeared on his face. "Um…he likes to jump on the bed, and I let him…sometimes."

"That was a pretty loud thump."

"Yeah, he likes to put his beanbags on the floor and…" Another thump sounded, and Carly flinched.

"…jump from the bed to the beanbags," she finished for him.

He shrugged. "Yep."

"Okay. That's good information to have. However—" she looked at Mason "—why don't you go check to make sure?" He nodded and left. Carly paced to the kitchen and back then shot a glance at Nick. "That's sweet of you to let him do something most parents would yell about."

Another guilty flush appeared, and he looked away. Inspiration hit her. "You do it, too, don't you?"

He raised a brow, going for the innocent look. "What do you mean?"

"Oh, no, you don't, Nicholas Floyd, you don't fool me." She shook a finger at him. "Not only do you do it, too, I bet you taught him!"

Nick shoved his hands into his pockets, and Carly swore he was hiding a grin. "Well, I…"

Carly crossed her arms and put on her stern look. "Come on, Judge, how do you plead?"

He let out a sigh and the little-boy look on his face tugged at her heartstrings. "Guilty as charged, ma'am."

Carly felt her heart thaw about ten degrees. She sobered and looked into his eyes, thought about asking him about the murderer he'd let go. No not now, she decided.

Nicholas placed a hand on her arm, and she felt the touch clear to her toes. She turned a questioning look at him, as he said, "Thank you."

"For what?"

"For everything. For not giving me a hard time about not hiding out and leaving the bad guys to you."

Crossing her arms over her middle, Carly zeroed in on his eyes. "Yeah, about that. We're going to have to have a little heart-to-heart about some of those rules we kind of skipped over earlier."

FOUR

Nick raised a brow. "Let me check on the kids, and then we can talk." He didn't really need to check on them. He knew Debbie would take good care of them; however, their frightened faces wouldn't leave his mind, and he needed to spend a little time reassuring them.

Carly nodded, and he headed upstairs to find Debbie sitting on the bed with Christopher in her lap. "I'll take it from here."

Debbie smiled and kissed the top of the boy's head then scooted out from under him. "'Night, Chris."

"'Night, Debbie."

Nick placed a hand on her arm and said, "I appreciate your help. But I think it might be best if you went home until all of this is resolved."

"But Nick…"

"I mean it, Debbie. I don't want you in danger. Tonight just proved that these guys don't care who's around when they come after me. It's not safe."

She chewed her bottom lip, and her brows dipped in a hesitant frown. She glanced at Christopher then back at Nick. "All right, maybe you're right. I guess—"

"No! No, she can't leave!"

The cry came from the bed as Christopher shot straight up in protest.

Running feet sounded on the steps from outside the room. Nick stepped out of the bedroom and saw Carly at the landing, gun drawn. He waved her down and turned back to Christopher.

Grabbing the little boy up in his arms, he hugged him. Christopher snagged him around the neck and squeezed. "Please don't make her leave, Uncle Nick, please."

Nick's heart nearly ruptured with a love so intense he had to close his eyes to gain control of his voice. Finally he said, "It's okay, Christopher. I've got you."

Still keeping his arms looped around his uncle's neck, Christopher pulled back to look into Nick's eyes. "I want Miss Debbie to stay. I need her. She makes me not be so scared."

"Nick…" Debbie laid a hand on his shoulder, and he glanced up into her beseeching eyes. She licked her lips and said, "Let me stay. The kids have had enough." She looked at Carly standing in the door and taking in the scene. "We've got protection. The kids need me…."

Nick pulled in a deep breath and shot a glance at Carly. She lifted a brow and gave a shrug as though to say it was up to him.

Debbie said, "And anyway, if they knew enough to find the generator, they probably know that I'm the nanny. They probably know a lot more than we think. What if they've been watching…" She paused and drew in a deep breath, her eyes cutting to the children. "If I leave, will they come after me even though I wouldn't technically be employed here anymore?"

Carly rubbed her nose and looked at Nick. He blinked. "That's a good question. What do you think, Carly?"

"I think she's probably right. Her safest place might just be right here."

Christopher relaxed against him. "Then she's staying, right?"

Nick kissed the freckled cheek. "Yeah, little man, it looks like she's staying."

"Good. I can go to sleep now."

Nicholas tucked the child in and escorted the two ladies from the room. Once back downstairs, he looked at Carly and said, "The only way to stop these people is not to give in to them. If I hand this case over to Debbie's father, I'm just going to be passing the danger on to him. Or anyone else who takes it."

"But it would take the danger off the kids, Nick. My dad isn't afraid. He'd do it for your kids." Debbie's soft voice penetrated his muddled thoughts.

"They're not after the kids. They're after me."

"What if the kids get caught in the crossfire?" Debbie persisted. Carly stayed quiet, and he couldn't tell what she thought.

Maybe Debbie was right. Even though the children hadn't been openly threatened, who knew if that would change?

"What if I sent them away? Somewhere safe?"

Carly frowned at him. "Where would you send them?"

Before he could answer, a low voice said, "No. I don't want to be sent anywhere."

Nick closed his eyes then opened them and turned to see Lindsey standing on the top stair, staring down at them. Her attitude was gone. In its place was a scared little girl. Lower lip trembling, she begged, "Don't send us away, Uncle Nick. We'll be safe with you."

Nick bit back a groan and resisted the urge to grab his

hair in both fists. What to do? Usually, decisions came easily to him. But this…the safety of the kids, the integrity of the case…

What should he do?

"I don't think it would help to send them away," Carly said. "There's no guarantee they wouldn't be followed or tracked down." She shook her head. "No, it's best they stay here where we can keep an eye on them. Besides—" she lowered her voice "—you and Debbie are their security right now. I don't think it would be a good idea to take that away. Like you said, you're the target, not them."

Nick breathed a sigh of relief, and Lindsey shot Carly a grateful look.

He hated to admit he hadn't wanted to be the one to make the decision. Uproot them and send them away and disrupt their young lives once more—even more so than having two U.S. Marshals move in—and have danger track them down. Or keep them here where danger might be just around the corner.

No, not a decision he was comfortable with either way.

He said, "If you can keep them safe, I'd prefer they stay here."

She looked him in the eye. "Whoever is after you will have to go through me to get to them."

Nicholas wasn't surprised at Carly's calm declaration. No, he was startled by his own reaction—that if it came down to her being in the line of fire, he'd make sure he was around to get her out of the way.

That settled, Carly swept past everyone and into the nearest bathroom off the kitchen. She fought the swirl of nausea in the pit of her stomach and gripped the sides of the sink.

She'd just promised to keep Lindsey and Christopher safe, and she had no idea who had just breached their defenses. Who? How? And what was she going to do about it?

She wanted to pray, ask for guidance, strength and protection, and yet she no longer felt that God was a resource for her. After Hank, her partner, mentor and friend, had been killed so senselessly, she'd thrown her hands up and told God she was done with Him because He never seemed to intervene when it was most needed. So why bother with Him?

"Why bother?" she whispered.

Turning on the cold water, she cupped her hands and splashed her face. Using the lightly scented hand towel, she dried off and stared at herself in the mirror. "You can do this," she whispered. "You don't need God or anyone else. This is your job. You're good at it. So do it." She narrowed her eyes. "And no romantic feelings for the judge, got it?"

Unfortunately, she didn't think her heart was listening.

The knock on the door startled her, and she called, "Be right there."

With one more look in the mirror, she decided she was presentable. She opened the door to find her partner on the phone. He hung up and asked, "Are you all right?"

"Yeah."

Curiosity lit his eyes, and for a moment she thought he was going to ask more questions, but he didn't, just shrugged and motioned her out of the bathroom.

"Is everything okay?" Nick asked from the doorway of the kitchen.

Carly forced a smile. "Everything's fine. Are you ready to go over some of those rules?"

"Sure." He gestured to one of the chairs at the kitchen table.

Mason said, "While you two do that, I'm going to patrol the grounds one more time."

He left, and Carly sat on the cushioned seat. She leaned back into the wood slats that made up the back of the chair. "First of all, are the kids asleep?"

"Yes, from what I can tell. Debbie said she'd keep an eye on them for the next hour or so."

"Okay, I'm thinking it might be a good idea to keep them home from school until all this is over."

Nick frowned. "Don't you have two other marshals on them?"

"Yes, Maria and Grady."

He shook his head and reached up to rub a hand across his lips as he thought. "No, as long as it's safe, they need the consistency. I'll drive them to school tomorrow, and Maria and Grady can stay on them like flypaper."

"Uh, I hate to tell you this, but you won't be driving anyone anywhere."

"Fine, you can, but I'm going with them."

"Nick, stop and think a minute…."

He lasered her with an unwavering stare. "I mean it. They'd go nuts around here with nothing to do but worry about whether or not someone is going to kill me. They're not the targets—I am." He thought for a moment. "If they're separate from me, they may be safe, right?"

"Yes. That's why sending them away would be a good thing in that sense. Yet Lindsey's reaction to that suggestion was very strong. Until it becomes a matter of us feeling unable to keep them safe in your presence, then…"

He blew out a sigh and looked at the ceiling. "All right. I'll agree to riding behind in a separate car, but I want to see them safely delivered. Plus, I need to have a few words with their teachers."

She wasn't going to change his mind. She'd convince him later that he didn't need to talk to the teachers. The marshals would take care of that. For now, she let the subject drop instead of arguing with the man.

Stubborn man. Likeable man. Strangely admirable man. Her brain flashed a yellow caution sign. Was that respect she was feeling for him? But what about Hank's killer? The one he'd set free….

Emotions twisting inside her like a balloon in a windstorm, she bit her lip. She sighed. "Fine. Then I'll be driving."

He gave her a gentle smile. "I figured."

Her heart stuttered in response, and she cleared her throat and debated whether or not to say what she was thinking.

His eyes narrowed. "What?"

A flush started at the base of her neck. She felt the heat rise to her cheeks then decided to be honest. "I'm…torn. On the one hand, it's good to see you again, Nick. Then again, it's not. Two years ago, I thought I'd made a friend in you. I respected you. Then when you let Hank's killer off on a technicality… I have to admit, I'm struggling with that one."

Nicholas sat back, stretched his legs out in front of him and crossed his ankles. He looked down at the table then back up to meet her eyes. "I wondered when you'd feel like talking about it."

"I don't really feel like it, but maybe we should."

He reached over and grasped her hand in his. Almost absently, he twined his fingers through hers. Bolts of awareness shot through her, and she swallowed hard. Why was she so attracted to this man? She didn't remember this feeling from two years ago. Of course, he had been married then… She would never let herself have any feelings toward a married man. Now, however, it seemed there was some kind of pull between them.

He was saying, "It wasn't something I wanted to do, Carly. You have to know that. When Ritchie Hardin appeared in my court that first time for armed robbery, I was ready to put him away for a long time. But his lawyer had irrefutable evidence that the police had messed up the case. I didn't want to let Hardin go, but my hands were tied."

With a finger on her free hand, she tapped her forehead. "I think I know that here." She moved her finger to touch the area above her heart. "It's here that's having the trouble. Hank taught me so much about being a good marshal, it just tears me up inside that he died because he was in the wrong place at the wrong time." She shook her head. "If he just hadn't walked into that store the day you released Hardin, Hardin wouldn't have been able to follow him to his granddaughter's ballet recital…" She blew out a breath. "It's just wrong." She palmed a tear, then looked away to compose herself.

He nodded then offered a small sad smile. "I know. I agree with you." A moment of silence, then, "For the record, it's good to see you again, too. I've often thought of our late-night chats from two years ago."

"Really?" That surprised her. She would have thought he'd have been relieved to be rid of her. He hadn't been keen on the idea of protection in the first place. His wife had practically disappeared into the bedroom while she and Mason had been in their house.

"Absolutely," he said. "I'm sure you could tell my marriage wasn't exactly…um…perfect."

Uncomfortable, wondering where he was going with

this line of conversation, Carly shifted. But didn't pull her hand from his. And he didn't let it go. "Yeah, I kind of got that feeling."

"We'd been fighting for days. You see, Miriam desperately wanted a child. And we just couldn't get pregnant in spite of doing everything medically possible. I told her I was done with doctors and treatments and wanted to talk about adoption. She was furious, wouldn't listen to a word I had to say. She finally decided on the silent treatment a couple of hours before your arrival."

"I'm sorry." So that explained his wife's disappearing act.

He pinched the bridge of his nose. "Me, too. As for letting a killer go, I did what I had to do. The officer in charge of the case was lax." His jaw clenched, and his eyes narrowed at her. "He let there be a possibility of tainted evidence. I didn't want to let Richie Hardin go. I did everything short of planting evidence myself to keep him behind bars, where I knew he belonged. Please believe me, but—"

A flicker from beyond the kitchen window caught her attention, and she straightened. "What was that?"

"What?"

Ignoring his sudden tension, she freed her hand from his and got on the radio. "Mason, did you see that?"

Her partner's voice came into her ear loud and clear. "See what?"

"There was a light, a flash of something outside the kitchen on the south side."

"I didn't see it, but I heard something coming from that direction. I was just getting ready to check it out when you called. Making my way around there now."

She stood and motioned for Nick to follow her. "I

need you to get in a safe place. Away from windows and doors."

"Surely they wouldn't try anything again tonight, would they?" He walked toward the stairs as he talked.

"Why not? It's what I'd do. Hit them again while they're off guard and recovering." She checked her weapon. "Just stay there on the steps, about midway up. You should be fine there until we figure out what's making those flashes."

"Could they be communicating that way?"

"Possibly. Although with today's technology, that'd be kind of dumb, if you ask me."

"Unless they're afraid we'll pick up on their signal."

"True." She didn't tell him she'd already thought of that. Radioing for backup once again, she made her way to the French doors that led to the patio. "Mason?"

"I'm not seeing—" he broke off as the flash came again. This time a little brighter—and a little closer. "Saw it."

"Can you tell where it's coming from? Is anyone answering it?"

"I'm headed in that direction. You stay with the family."

Carly bit back a protest. He was right. She was where she was needed. "Come on, Nick, into the stairwell."

"Fine, but you stay nearby."

She knew he wasn't asking for her presence out of safety concerns. He wanted to know what was going on as soon as she did.

"I need to check upstairs. You stay put."

"I'll be right behind you."

Frustration nearly made her scream. Clamping her lips together, she refused to let it out and quietly made her way up the stairs to the kids' rooms. Christopher lay sprawled on his back across the twin bed, covers bunched around his waist.

Nick straightened them, then bent down and pressed an ear to the boy's chest. He listened for a few seconds, closed his eyes and whispered something Carly took to be a prayer.

Then he was towering over her once more. "Lindsey's room?"

She nodded silently, ear tuned for the slightest out-of-place sound. He padded down the hall to the next room. Opening the door, they found Debbie sitting on the bed, head against the wall, snoring gently. Lindsey had fallen asleep with her hand in Debbie's.

Carly's heart pinged. Poor kids. They didn't deserve this.

Nick's tension radiated. He held himself stiff, and she knew he wanted to run from the house, find whoever was doing this to his family and beat them senseless. That was okay. As long as he controlled himself.

"Mason?" she whispered into the radio. "What do you have?"

"False alarm."

Tension melted from her shoulders. "What was it?"

"Firecrackers."

"Kids getting ready for the Fourth?"

"Looks that way. I'm heading back to the house."

"See you in a few."

She looked at Nick. "False alarm. Just some kids setting off firecrackers."

Relief rolled across his face. "Now what?"

"Get some sleep. Morning's coming early."

FIVE

Nick hit the ground running early the next morning. After a heated twenty-minute discussion, Carly talked him into making a phone call to the principal instead of going on school grounds.

"The minute you set foot on that campus, you're putting every child in danger," she insisted. "These people didn't care that you had two children in your house when they came to get you last night. They won't care if you're surrounded by children. You don't need to be anywhere near them."

Nick had paused, thought about it and reluctantly seen the wisdom of her words.

Letting the kids go to school—having them out of his sight—wasn't an easy task, even though he knew it was probably best for them. Familiar surroundings, keeping their minds occupied.

And not in his presence.

Yes, best for them, but he really didn't want them to go. In fact, he almost changed his mind—twice.

But Lindsey seemed to perk up at the thought of going. She was in a small class play and had had her costume ready for weeks. When he'd suggested she might have to skip it, she'd gone nuts—and the hurt in her eyes had broken his heart.

Although if he thought she'd be in danger at the school, he'd live with the broken heart.

And Christopher couldn't wait to tell his teacher about the "cool cops" living in his house.

Nick made the call, reassuring the principal and the school resource officer that extreme security measures would be taken to ensure no one at the school was in any danger at any time. No threats had been made against the children, just Nick.

Extra officers would patrol the grounds and be on hand should they be needed. Nick didn't think they would. The de Lugos wanted him off the case or dead. They had no reason to go after the children.

Except to use them as incentive to get him to recuse himself, delay the trial, give them time to come up with more fabricated evidence and fake alibis.

Those thoughts disturbed him enough that he hesitated again. However, Grady and Maria were right there with them. This was what the marshals were trained for. The children would be fine.

Satisfied that he'd covered all his bases and the children would be safe, escorted to and from school by the two other marshals, Nick watched them enter the building from the safety of the car. Carly had parked off-campus, on a hill that afforded them a view of the school's front door.

She sat in the driver's seat, having insisted upon driving. That was fine with him. It gave him time to think about the situation he now found himself in.

Sometimes he wondered why he'd ever switched out of family court, but then he thought about the de Lugo family and his resolve hardened. Someone had to stand up to those who thought they were above the law.

In the police academy it hadn't taken him long to get frustrated with the system, which was why he'd made the transition to law school. He'd thought he could do more as a judge, help the officers who made the arrests and make their job a little easier, a little more satisfactory.

He wasn't sure if he'd been successful or not.

But it didn't mean he was ready to give up.

"Are you sure this is the right thing, Nick?"

"What do you mean?" He knew what she meant, but he found he liked the sound of her voice. He wanted to hear it over the confusion in his mind. Wanted her to explain in that soft, lilting tone she used sometimes.

She hesitated then asked, "Is it worth it? Putting your life on the line? Possibly those kids' lives, to keep this case?"

Being a judge, dedicating his life to justice, helping those who couldn't help themselves. That was his job, his life— his calling.

And he told her so.

"Besides—" his jaw firmed as he spoke "—if I let them get to me, if I allow myself to be scared into passing the case on to someone else, a judge who doesn't have the same values as I do might be inclined to be swayed or lenient. What would that say to all the other criminals out there? *Threaten the judge you don't like and get the one you do?* Or that it's okay to harass and threaten until the case is dropped because no judge will go up against them? Then there's always the trick of significantly delaying the trial in order to buy enough time to fabricate evidence to dispute the real evidence against you." He shook his head. "I can't let that happen. I can't be the one to put that kind of power into their hands."

Respect blipped in her eyes, and he appreciated that she didn't seem to judge *that* decision. He knew it might sound cold, that it might appear that he was putting his career before the safety of his family, but that wasn't it. "Do you understand why I can't give in? I'm not being stubborn. I'm not doing this just to get scum off the street, but to show those kids you don't let intimidation scare you away from doing what's right. You do the best you can to keep yourself safe, and then you go ahead and do the right thing."

"You don't have to justify yourself to me, Nick." Her voice was soft velvet that shimmered over him, made him glad he'd trusted her with a little bit of his convictions.

It made him willing to open up a little further. He added, "I'll be honest. After Miriam and my sister died in the wreck, I questioned that. I questioned everything. For about a month, I just fell apart. I couldn't focus, couldn't think. I didn't want to get out of bed in the morning."

"Understandable." Compassion coated the word.

"For a while, yes. By this time I had the kids living with me. Mom took care of them." He gave a humorless laugh. "Actually, she took care of everything. I was so lost in my grief, I couldn't see the toll her own grief was taking." He blew out a sigh. "And I certainly didn't see how badly the kids were hurting."

"You can't blame yourself for that."

He sighed. "Yes, I can. I took a month off work...life. Took a sabbatical to the mountains to do some soul-searching. Faith-searching."

"What did you find out?"

"That I felt more guilt than grief over my wife's death."

"Guilt?"

He flushed, wondered how much to tell her. Then settled for saying, "Because I was more passionate about my job than I was about my marriage."

Empathy flashed, and she covered his hand with hers.

He felt a zing, one he realized he was beginning to feel whenever he came into contact with her. He wondered about it, wanted to explore it, even as he did his best to push it away.

Then he was distracted by her lips tugging upward in a wry smile. "Why do you think I'm still single at the ripe old age of thirty-three?"

Before he could think of what to say to that, her eyes shifted then narrowed, and he knew she was listening to the voice in her earpiece. Then she said, "Copy that."

He cleared his throat and decided to move away from personal stuff. "So, do I get to go to work now?"

Cranking the car, she shifted it into gear and slid away from the curb. "As soon as the SWAT team gets into place."

Nick had been a judge for years, and no one had ever made such a fuss about his safety. "A SWAT team? Are you serious?"

"It's just a precaution. These people have already infiltrated your home. It only makes sense that they're going to come after you at work. Since I can't talk you into staying home, this is the next best thing."

He paused. Should he consider staying home? The de Lugo case was just under a week away. Should he go ahead and hide out until then? Everything in him shouted out in protest. The practical side of him came up with a mental checklist of pros and cons.

Pro: He could distribute the remaining cases on his docket without much trouble. Wayne could take a few, as could Sebastian Michaels, one of the other judges who shared in the rotation.

Con: It might send the wrong message to the children, i.e., if you're threatened, tuck your tail and run.

Pro: Or it might teach them to assess the situation, recognize they need help and do the smart thing.

Nick sighed. But was it the smart thing to do? Was it necessary?

He had to admit it might be. Then again, he did have help. U.S. Marshals who were very good at their jobs.

"Nick?"

He blinked, her voice pulling him from his thoughts. "Huh?"

"I said we're ready. We've swept the courthouse, and there are SWAT members scattered around the rooftops. Also, the media is in a frenzy. Keep your head low and don't say a word to anyone."

He didn't move for a brief moment. Then he said, "All right. Let's do it. I'll get the files I need, but then we'll play it your way. Although it goes against everything in me, we'll go to a safe house and hide out."

"I really do think that would be best. While I don't think the kids are in any immediate danger, that could change in the blink of an eye. We want to take preventive measures instead of having to react to an emergency. I'll notify the two marshals guarding them of the change in plans."

He reached up to rub his eyes in a weary gesture. "Lindsey's going to be furious about missing all of the end-of-school activities."

"At least she'll be alive to get over it."

Carly pulled around to the back of the courthouse only to find it jammed with protestors holding signs and yelling the occasional comment to anyone who would listen. The media covered the area, eating up the conflict and occasional outbreak of violence.

Local police had things under control.

For now.

A little less than a week before the trial, and it had already started. Ricardo de Lugo may be a mobster, but he also funded numerous charitable organizations and did his best to put up a respectable front.

Most unaware citizens fell for his charade and were now outraged that he'd been arrested.

Law enforcement knew the truth.

After flashing her badge to the security guard, Carly pulled into the underground parking garage where the general public was blocked from entering. "Let's get what you need and get out. That crowd looks like it could turn very nasty at any moment."

"Fine. I just need to get into my office."

Another car pulled into the spot beside Carly's, and Mason climbed out.

"This shouldn't take long."

Mason nodded. "You two go ahead. I'll bring up the rear."

With Carly in the front, Nick behind her and Mason keeping watch behind him, the three made their way into the building and down the hall.

A lone janitor ran a mop across the floor. Two security guards patrolled inside.

Carly took in the details, registering them in her mind even as her eyes swept side halls and closed doors.

Finally, they came to the door that opened into his secretary's area. Stepping inside, led the way past the empty desk. Then stopped. "Where's your secretary?"

A frown furrowed his brow. "I don't know. She's usually here by the time I get here—and that's when I'm on time. Today I'm unusually late."

Carly looked at Mason, and he said, "I'll find her." Before he could get on the phone, a figure entered and came to an abrupt halt.

"Oh, Judge Floyd, there you are." The slender, fifty-something woman looked at each person invading her space. Then she said, "Is something wrong?"

Nick took the lead. "I'm going to be out of the office for a while, Jean. I just need to get some files, and then I'll be out of your hair."

She blinked at him, clearly dumbfounded. "Out of the office? When the de Lugo case is coming up? Are you out of your mind?"

Carly bit her lip in amusement at Nick's consternation and waited for him to explain. He blew out a breath and said, "I need to take my family somewhere safe until the trial...."

Realization dawned on her features. "You're going into hiding because of the threats."

She was sharp. Of course, she'd been questioned about the letter he'd received yesterday. Was it just yesterday? It felt like a lifetime.

Nick nodded. "Yes." He waved toward Carly and Mason. "These are two U.S. Marshals assigned to keep me safe until the trial." He made the introductions, and Jean smiled and shook their hands. "They want me in a safer place than this." He paused and shrugged. "And because of the kids, I'm taking the advice of the professionals."

His secretary nodded, her salt-and-pepper bun bobbing. "Good. What files do you need? I'll be glad to get them for you."

Nick held up a hand. "No, I know exactly where everything is. I'll get them. And I'll be accessible." He looked at Mason. "Can you give Jean a number to call in case she needs to get in touch with me?"

Mason hesitated. "It might be better if you just call from my encrypted cell phone on a regular basis to check in.

That way if someone questions her, she can honestly say she can't get in touch with you."

Nick said, "But if you're pushed or feel threatened in any way, you let them know that I'll be calling in, all right?"

Her eyes narrowed, and she waved a hand. "All right, then. Now, if you don't need me, I'm going to get some coffee. After my wild-goose chase this morning, I need some caffeine."

Carly perked up. "Wild-goose chase?"

"Someone from security called and told me I needed to sign some papers. When I got down there, no one seemed to know what I was talking about—said they must have dialed the wrong extension." She rolled her eyes. "Like I have time for that kind of thing."

Carly looked at the closed door straight ahead. Nick's office. And his secretary had been called away from her desk on a wild-goose chase.

Leaving the office available for entry by anyone who walked by.

And decided to lie in wait?

She shot a look at Mason and held out a hand to Nick. "Key?"

With a sigh, Nick handed the ring over, separating one key and letting the rest dangle from the key chain.

Eyeing him, she said, "Will you please stay out here? You're the target. Let's not give them something to aim at."

She could tell he didn't like it, the conflicted look in his eyes a clear indication that he wanted to rush in and confront whatever danger might be in there.

But he wouldn't.

And she appreciated that.

Pulse pounding, Carly took the key from him with one hand and inserted the key into the lock. She pulled her weapon with the other hand. Nothing had set off her internal alarm, but it never hurt to be prepared. She noticed Mason had his gun ready, too.

A quick twist opened the door, and she stepped inside, eyes scanning the room.

Empty.

"Clear," she called. Then the heat hit her. "Why is it so hot in here?"

Nick and Mason followed her through the door. Before she could say anything, Mason pointed for Nick to stay back against the wall. Mason shut the door behind him. "Stay there while I check the bathroom."

Nick grunted. "Is the air-conditioning working?"

Mason crossed the room to the bathroom, looked in and said, "Clear."

Nick immediately headed to check the thermostat on the wall. "It's been cranked up to eighty-five degrees." He readjusted it. "Remind me to ask Jean what that was all about." He switched to business mode. "I'll need that laptop," he said, pointing to his desk.

"Uh, not clear," Mason called in quiet voice. "I've got a snake in here."

"A snake? Are you sure?" She walked to the desk to get the laptop. "Do you need help?"

"Probably. It's a rattler. Be on the lookout out there in case he's got company."

In the process of powering down the computer, Carly froze as she heard a slight hiss by her foot. She almost jerked away before she saw movement on the floor in front of the desk. Then she went still.

Very, very still.

Nick reached for the file cabinet. "Nick." She kept her voice soft, low. He turned at the intensity, his hand hovering above the handle to the first drawer.

His eyes narrowed as he took in her completely still state. "What is it?"

"There's one under the desk." She felt the movement of the air near her calf. It was that close. She couldn't help the slight tremor that shuddered through her. At any moment she expected to feel sharp fangs sink into her leg. "It could strike at any moment if I move. Get out of here, Nick."

Nick blanched. "Not a chance. I'm not leaving you guys to face this alone."

Mason looked over his shoulder as he backed from the entrance to the bathroom. "I think there's more than one in here, too. I see a tail behind the toilet. Another one is on the light fixture up above."

In seconds Nick was on the phone with security explaining the situation—and the need for Animal Control—or an exterminator. And he needed it now. Within minutes or heads would roll. He never took his eyes from Carly.

Carly felt the reptile's tongue flick in and out by her ankle. Wishing she had boots on, she didn't dare look down. Would the pounding of her heart cause the snake to strike? Could it feel the blood surging through her veins? Then she spotted the one in front of the desk moving across the floor toward Nicholas.

"Nick," she whispered, desperate to warn him but not do anything to set off the snake by her leg, "over there. Watch out."

Mason had grabbed a towel from the rack and closed the bathroom door. He stuffed the towel into the crack at the bottom of the door while Nick moved toward Carly, a respectful eye on the snake headed toward the file cabinet.

"Stay away," she whispered. "Don't get any closer to it. They're attracted to movement." With willpower she didn't realize she possessed, she ignored the fear cramping her stomach and reasoned that if she was bitten, she was only a few blocks from the hospital, where a few vials of antivenom would fix her right up.

A rattle sounded, and Carly sucked in a deep breath. Something had triggered the alarm of the one across the floor. Probably the vibrations of Nick's footsteps. It now lay coiled and ready to strike.

The one cozying up to her foot was still there. She closed her eyes. *Don't look, don't look.*

"I'm here. I'm not going to let him bite you."

"Nick, these were meant for you. Get away." She kept her voice low, barely pushing the words past lips that didn't want to move.

"Not a chance."

A knock sounded on the door. "Animal Control."

The coiled snake in the middle of the floor twitched and curled tighter, its tail shaking ferociously.

Nick grabbed the nearest trash can and moved toward the snake on the floor. "Everyone just stay still." Carly watched him focus on the snake, knowing his timing had to be perfect. She looked at the snake's eyes. For some reason she remembered that science lesson on how to tell a poisonous snake from a nonpoisonous.

By their eyes. Round equaled nonpoisonous. Slanted equaled poisonous.

This snake definitely had slanted eyes. It was poisonous. Of course, the rattle had been the big clue.

Nick moved closer.

"Be careful, Nick," Carly whispered to his back.

Closer.

The snake reared its head back, and Nick dropped the trash can. The sound of its head striking the metal reverberated through the room. On silent feet, he moved to the door and opened it.

Two men in protective gear entered. Nick said, "Get the one away from her first."

They took in the scenario, and the one on the right said, "So this is the emergency. Wow." Sucking in a deep breath, he said, "I'm Brad. This is Joe. How many?"

Nick exchanged a look with Mason, who whispered, "Two in the bathroom. Two—that we know of—out here. One of the two is under the trash can. The other is right by her leg."

Joe approached Carly. He held a tool in his right hand. "Ma'am, just keep still."

She flashed him a just-shut-up-and-hurry look. He got the message and held the tool out in front of him. In a soft voice, he explained, "These are snake tongs, ma'am. Basically, I'm going to use the clamp on the end to grab him, all right?"

"Fine," she whispered. "Just do it."

"Just stay still. If you move…"

Carly glared at him and sucked in a breath. "Right."

The tongs reached out toward the head of the snake as it bobbed. The tongue flickered as the man made a gentle motion away from Carly's leg and the snake turned its attention toward the tongs.

Everyone stood statue still.

The tongs opened, operated by the squeeze handle. Then Joe pulled back. "I…I'm sorry. I can't do it. I'm new, and I'm afraid…" Sweat poured down his face and into his eyes as he licked his lips, gaze darting between Carly and the snake.

"Give me the tongs." Brad snatched them from his partner and turned to Carly. "You ready?"

"Just get this thing away from me. Now!" she hissed.

Brad nodded and copied Joe's earlier move, holding the tongs over the head of the snake. Once again, the reptile bobbed close, tongue flicking at the motion.

Then in one lightning-fast move, Brad clamped the tongs around the base of the snake's head. She felt it try to lunge briefly toward her leg, but before she could even think about reacting, he had the reptile in the bag he'd brought with him.

Carly's knees weakened, but she couldn't collapse yet. There might be more where those came from.

Fortunately, there weren't.

Thirty minutes later, the office was declared reptile-free. Now came the process of figuring out who had placed them there—and how.

Nicholas watched the surveillance video from the safety of the security room located in the back of the courthouse. "A lot of activity. A lot of security. How did he get in with a bag of snakes?"

Anger burned inside of him. Carly had almost been bitten. Granted, she might not have died, but she would have been dreadfully sick. Out of commission for a while. Because of him. Because of his job.

Just like his wife and sister. Possibly dead because of his job. At least, that was what he told himself. Because in spite of the fact that the police investigator had ruled it an accident, Nick had never been completely convinced.

He recalled the facts. A one-car accident on a rainy night. No evidence of foul play. The only skid marks had belonged to the Honda Pilot Miriam had been driving with his sister in the passenger seat.

The car Nick usually drove.

But why had she been going so fast, only to slam on the brakes and hydroplane off the road, colliding viciously with a telephone pole?

Miriam hated to speed. He used to tease her about being a "grandma" driver.

For her to have been going that fast… The only explanation he could come up with was that she was running from someone. She'd been scared. As a result, she'd wrecked and the two women had died.

That was no accident in Nick's book. That was murder.

But he had no proof, just a gut feeling. That hadn't been enough to convince the authorities. If he were honest, he couldn't blame them.

Finally, he'd called in a favor from a detective on the force. The man looked into it and declared he couldn't find any evidence that indicated it was anything but an accident.

"Of course, the physical evidence of the accident is gone, but after examining the photos and written reports… I'm sorry, Nick. It really looks like an accident."

But Nick knew in his gut it wasn't.

Just like the snakes in his office weren't an accident. No, they were a message. One he got loud and clear. He shuddered. What if he'd had the kids with him? Or what if his secretary had entered for some reason?

These people were ruthless.

And it made him that much more determined to put them away for as long as possible.

Quitting wasn't in his vocabulary, and the sooner they realized that, the faster this would all be over.

He prayed that was the case, anyway.

A phone rang. The officer next to Nicholas snatched his cell phone from the clip on his belt. He listened. Then his face went pale. "We'll be right there."

He hung up, his fingers fumbling with the device as he placed it back in the clip. "I think I know how the snakes got in."

SIX

Carly stared down at the body of the security guard. Anger filled her at the senseless killing. He'd been shot in the head, stripped of his uniform and tossed into the bathroom stall like yesterday's garbage. Again, the thought crossed her mind. Why kill him and not leave something like a bomb in Nick's office, since they had access to it? Why snakes? The snakes must have been more of a warning than an attempt to kill.

So, what was the attack on the house? Another message? A true try at killing him? Or something else? Carly's brain processed these thoughts as Nick slammed a fist against the wall and muttered something she couldn't hear. If he was praying, she hoped somebody was listening.

"Another example of complete and utter disregard for human life," she muttered. Nicholas looked like granite. Trying to read his expression was like staring at a blank page. "Nick? What are you thinking?"

"That I want these people stopped, and I want them stopped yesterday."

"We're working on that."

His face softened slightly. "I know."

The crime-scene unit arrived, and Carly stepped back. Mason pulled out his phone and started barking orders.

Nick placed a hand on her arm, and she looked up at him. His touch sent a shiver up her shoulder. Clearing her throat, she asked, "Are you ready to head to the safe house now?"

He blew out a sigh and transferred the hand on her arm to grasp the bridge of his nose with two fingers. "Yes, I think we're going to have to drop out of sight in order to keep people alive. I don't like it. I don't like being forced into—" He broke off and shook his head. "Well, no sense grumbling about it. We'll do what we've got to do, and that's that."

She was quiet for a moment. "They had this planned."

"What?"

"This was all planned. It had to be. How did they know you were going to be here today?"

He shot her a wry look. "I'm always here, Carly. Unfortunately, my schedule isn't one that I can alter very much. I might drive a different route to work or come in a little early on Monday, leave late on Tuesday, and so on, but for the most part, I'm here at this time of day. Anyone who knows me…or has been watching me…wouldn't have much trouble figuring that out."

She frowned. "Okay. Point taken. But to be ready to act so fast."

Mason walked up in time to hear her comment, and all three headed back to the security room. "They must have had someone watching the courthouse. Waiting for the judge to arrive. All it takes is a phone call. Then the guy pops the first security guard that comes his way, and the game is on."

"And with all of the hoopla it took to get in and park…"

"By the time we got in the building, the person had plenty of time to get the message and let the snakes in."

Nick's fingers curled into a fist. She watched his jaw clench, causing a muscle to jump. As he opened his mouth to say something, his cell phone rang.

Carly turned to Mason to suggest he check out the secretary's wild-goose chase while she and Nick finished the surveillance tapes.

"Excuse me?" Nick's deadly quiet question pulled her attention back to him.

He pressed a button on the iPhone screen to engage the speakerphone, and a mechanically disguised voice said, "You heard me, Judge. I have one of my men at your children's school. Watching them even as we speak. You think those two incompetent marshals can keep me from them if I want them?"

Mason grabbed his phone and stepped from the room. Carly knew he was calling Maria or Grady to alert them of the new developments.

Nick already had a trace on his phone. Every incoming and outgoing call would be recorded.

"You leave those kids out of this." Nick's face had gone pale even as stark determination stamped his features. "They've got nothing to do with any of this."

"Their mother and aunt didn't have anything to do with one of your cases, either, did they? And yet look where they ended up. You're messing with the same people, Judge, so you know how we work. Still want to take us on?"

Stunned, Carly drew in a swift breath and could only stare at Nick, her heart breaking at the harsh grief that stole his voice for a moment. Then he cleared his throat. "How do you know anything about that? Are you admitting to murdering my wife and sister?"

A harsh laugh echoed in the room. "You'd be surprised at what and who I know, what I've done—and what I'm capable of doing."

The words slammed into the air. Nick shot Carly a haunted look and spoke into the phone,. "If anything happens to those kids, I'll see you dead."

Another laugh. "Now, is that any way for a judge to talk?" The voice turned deadly. "I sent you a video. Either drop the case or be prepared to rule the way we want."

"I'll rule according to the evidence."

"That's what we figured. Watch the video, then decide. It might change your mind. Especially when you see the little bull's-eye on Lindsey's head."

The loud click of the caller hanging up spurred everyone into motion.

Carly hit the door to find Mason pacing, his phone stuck to his ear. She got his attention. "Did you get a trace?"

In disgust, he shook his head. "They covered their tracks."

She wasn't surprised. "What about Maria and Grady?"

"That's who I'm talking to now. Maria said Grady went with Christopher to class. She's with Lindsey and says everything is fine."

Carly looked back to see Nick standing in the doorway, listening. His relief was visible. She turned back to Mason. "This time the threat was made against the children. I want them away from that school."

"Working on it." He listened a few more moments. "They're all four together now. Grady's going to get the car while Maria stays with the kids in the shelter of the building."

"Good. Let's get more officers over there. Tell Maria and Grady to stay put until they see the cars—if they can."

"Carly? I need you to see this."

Nick's voice stopped her before she could issue the next order.

She turned to see that the pallor in his face had been replaced with a sickly green color.

She snatched the phone from his hand and pressed Play.

The children's school came into view, followed by video of the two marshals ushering Christopher and Lindsey into the building. The marshals blocked the view of the children, using their bodies as shields. She looked up at Nick, and he motioned her back to the phone. "Keep watching."

The next shot was through a window of one of the classrooms. Lindsey walked in, and for a brief moment, she was a target. Carly knew the person taking the video could have sent a bullet crashing through the glass into the girl.

Nausea curled through her as Maria rushed over to the window and pulled the blinds. Carly would have done that before Lindsey had walked into the classroom. Doing it now could have been too late if the person with the camera had a sharp shooting rifle instead.

"Okay, the kids have officially been threatened. No more school, no more regularly scheduled activities, until this trial is over," Carly said.

Her heart thumped and her breath caught in her throat at the dread she read on his face. She wanted to put her arms around him and offer him comfort. A fact that bothered her. She couldn't let her desire to grow close to Nick, the man, get in the way of her job, which was Nick the assignment. She was here for one thing and one thing only.

To keep him and his kids safe.

Any feelings she might have for him would have to be shelved.

"Mason, where are the kids now? Are they in the car yet?"

"Not yet. Maria's still waiting."

She frowned. "He's taking too long. He wouldn't have been parked that far from the entrance. Can she see him?"

Mason handed her the phone. "I don't know. Here, I'm going to make sure everything's arranged for the safe house. You take over."

Pressing the phone to her ear, she said, "Maria?"

"Yeah, something's going on. Grady shouldn't be taking this long."

"My thoughts exactly," Carly muttered. "Don't leave the kids. Give him a few more…"

"There he is." She could hear the relief in her fellow marshal's voice. "And two police cruisers just pulled into the parking lot."

"All right." Carly looked up as Mason walked back into the room. "Hang on a second, and I'll tell you which safe house."

Mason held up four fingers.

"Maria? Safe house number four."

"Got it."

"We'll meet you there. The cruisers will follow you and hold back traffic to make sure no one tails you to the safe house. You know the way."

She hung up.

Nick looked ready to explode. She forced reassurance into her tone. "The kids are fine, Nick. You'll be with them within thirty minutes. Debbie is being taken to the house as we speak, and the children will join her within minutes."

He paced from one end of the small room to the other. "I should have listened to you. I shouldn't have sent them to school. If something happens…"

She rested a hand on his arm, felt the tension radiating from the bunched muscles. "*Nothing* is going to happen."

He jerked away. "You don't know that."

Carly flinched as though he'd slapped her. He was right;

she didn't know that. After all, she'd thought Hank would pull through, had even laughed with him one last time before his heart stopped. Pulling in a calming breath, she said, "You're right. I don't. I..."

He held up a hand. "I'm sorry. I didn't mean to snap at you. I just want to see for myself."

"Absolutely. So let's get going."

Mason stepped back inside and motioned for them to follow him. Security coated the courthouse. The halls had been cleared. A police officer stood at each door, even the restrooms. They would make sure no one followed them out of the building. Mason, Carly and Nick would take the steps down to the parking garage. No elevators.

Mason led the way. Nick followed behind, and Carly brought up the rear.

Once in the garage, Mason got the car and brought it around. Carly and Nick hastened inside. Nick fastened his seat belt and asked, "Where is this safe house?"

Carly sat next to him in the backseat of the compact four-door car. Nick leaned toward her, his eyes intense, worry for the children visible. She felt something melt a little inside her when she saw the pain in his eyes.

"Just outside of town," she said soothingly.

Mason accelerated, and the bright sun hit them as they exited the garage.

Carly reached across the six inches separating Nick's hand from hers and placed her palm over his fingers. He jumped, that muscle in his jaw working once more.

But he didn't pull away.

Nick watched her flush, but she didn't take her hand from his grasp. "Carly?" He needed her to talk. He needed noise, a distraction—anything to keep him from dwelling on what could happen to the children if the marshals guarding them failed to protect them.

"Yeah?"

He barely heard her. "Are they safe with Maria and Grady? Would they put their lives on the line to protect them?" A pause. "Like you would?"

Her stormy blue eyes softened. "They're professionals, Nick. They'll do everything in their power to keep those kids safe, I promise. But—" she reached up to touch his cheek "—as soon as we have them back, we're not letting them out of our sight again, okay?"

We. Our. He liked her use of the possessive. Even as his heart climbed into his throat at the thought of what could happen to Lindsey and Christopher, having Carly by his side made all the difference in the world. "I need them to be safe," he whispered and bent his head to touch her forehead with his.

"I know," she whispered back. "And they will be. They *have* to be."

He pulled away and stared down at her, wondering what was happening between them, even in the midst of this crisis. He saw that if Carly's determination had anything to do with the children's safety, all would be well.

But he knew the killers were just as determined.

And that scared him more than he ever thought possible. "God is in control," he said. "They're in His care."

She jerked away from him and snorted, a new fire in her gaze. "I'm sorry, but just because you believe God will keep anything from happening to them doesn't make it so. If we want them safe, we, as in the marshals, will have to see to it."

For a moment, Nick felt extreme sadness. "Where's your faith, Carly?"

"Dead. As dead as Hank, my friend and mentor."

He winced as he felt her pain scorch his heart. "What would Ian say about that?"

She barked a laugh. "My brother says a whole lot about that when I give him the chance." A pause. "That's why I don't."

Then she turned her back on him, effectively telling him that she was done talking. Their intimate moment seemed to be a figment of his imagination, the comfort he'd derived from her closeness gone.

Fine. He pulled out his cell and called his housekeeper, Stella Jefferson. She answered on the first ring. "Hello, Nick."

He didn't spare any words. "We're going to have to go into a safe house. Do you and Carl want to join us or leave town for a while?"

"Oh, my." She sighed. "We'll leave. That'll be two less people to be protected, taking their attention from you and the children. Yes, we'll go to my sister's in Arizona. We'll be fine."

Emotion welled for his mother's friend. "Thank you for everything, I'll call when it's safe to come back."

"Take care, dear."

"You too."

Nick hung up, leaned back and stared at the ceiling, praying desperate prayers that the children would be fine. That everyone would stay safe until the criminals could be brought to justice.

Please, God.

Carly's phone rang, and she snatched it then fumbled with it, juggling it like a hot potato until she finally had it under control. "Hello?"

Nick studied her, wondering who it was. Then her face went pale; the sick look she shot him made his heart thud. "What?" he demanded. "What is it? The kids?"

She handed her phone to Mason and grabbed his from the cup holder. "Talk to Maria while I call for help." She shot Nick a compassionate look and dialed another number. "I need assistance at Old Gap Road and Silver Street. Officers down. Take a left up here, Mason."

Nick felt his heart freeze.

Mason shot her a look in the rearview mirror. "What is it, Carly?"

Nick grabbed her hand and demanded. "Tell me."

She swallowed once. Twice. "That was Maria. They've had a wreck. She's been shot, and Grady's… She thinks Grady's dead."

He forced the words past lips paralyzed with fear. "Christopher? Lindsey?"

"They're gone."

SEVEN

Nick sat in stone-faced silence the entire four minutes it took to get to the scene of the accident. Carly tried to order him to a secure area, but he'd stated he was going with or without her. She figured it would be safer for him to be there with her and Mason than to go off on his own.

Once they arrived, Carly took in the sight. One police cruiser had slammed into a tree. The officer in front lay unmoving across the steering wheel. The second cruiser had left skid marks, an obvious attempt to escape the bullets that had peppered the side.

Where was that officer? She couldn't see an outline through the window.

The marshals' vehicle didn't look good. The car lay on its side, the rear window completely shattered.

Cold chills swept through her. Someone had come prepared to take out bullet-resistant glass. *Oh, God, please.*

The prayer slipped through her mind, and, whether she wanted to admit it or not, it felt good, familiar, like talking to an old friend. Something to think about later.

They'd beaten backup there. Carly cased the area as Mason drove up to the edge, behind the marshal's battered car. Nick had his right hand on the door handle, ready to fling it open. She grabbed his left wrist, felt his pulse hammering under her fingertips. "Stay in the car, Nick. Please."

"I'm going to check on my kids."

"It may be a trap. Stay put." She could just picture him stepping out of the car and a sniper planting a bullet between his eyes. This was the perfect spot for it.

Trees lined the street on one side and buildings on the other. Plenty of hiding places all around.

"Mason, is Maria still on the line?"

"No, I lost her about a minute ago."

"She hung up?"

"I think she passed out."

Carly couldn't see anything through the tinted glass in the other car. Trees lined the edge of the road, and the woods beyond looked still, silent. Like they held secrets never to be revealed. She shook her head at herself. She knew better than to let her imagination take over.

The sound of a helicopter whirred above. She looked at Nick, who still had his hand on the handle. "Help's coming. I'll go check for the kids. You stay put."

His brow shot up. "I thought you said it might be a trap."

"A trap for *you*. They have no reason to shoot me."

The skepticism on his face said he didn't believe her. Well, that was all right. She wasn't sure she believed it herself.

Mason spoke from the driver's seat. "Carly, you know the drill. Don't do anything until the situation's been assessed and cleared."

"I've assessed it. I'm going to look for those children."

She was scared to death about the kids, and it sounded like Maria and Grady needed help, too.

Now.

She opened the door and slid out, her eyes probing every possible sniper hiding place.

"Carly…" The warning note in Mason's voice stopped her, and she looked back.

"Just keep your eyes open for me, will you?" she pleaded.

Steel fingers wrapped around her wrist and jerked her back into the car. Nick's hard eyes stared down at her. "Don't you dare. You follow protocol."

Speechless, she froze. What was that in his eyes? Fury? Fear? Yes, definitely fear. But something else, too. Disbelief at his nerve hammered her. "What are you doing?" she sputtered. "The kids…Maria…"

"He's right, Carly." Mason's hard voice and Nick's iron-clad hold on her made her shudder. The helicopter thumped louder. She knew it was doing a thermal scan of the woods. Soon, she would get the okay—if the shooter was gone.

But she was so mad, her hands shook. She needed to get to the car. Desperately. "Let me go," she ordered in a low voice. "The kids…I promised…"

Again, she tried to pull away, but Nick held fast. A noise in her ear distracted her, and she shoved her earpiece in, willing the pilot in the helicopter to give her the all-clear and to say he spotted two small figures.

The feel of Nick's strong fingers still wrapped around her wrist made her hesitate. She stopped, closed her eyes and took a deep breath. Why was she reacting this way? She'd had tough assignments before. Even ones involving children. Why was this case different? It shouldn't be. But it was. She'd been blindsided by her feelings. She realized she had come to care for this little family far more than she probably should.

Swallowing hard, she ordered herself to remain objective.

Right. She looked Nick in the eye and nodded. His fingers slid from her wrist as though in slow motion, his eyes never leaving her face.

Just as she registered the words in her ear, Mason shoved open his door. "I got the all clear," he said. "Two bodies that could be children spotted close by—one moving, one still, near the edge of the woods. No one carrying a weapon. We're good."

No one needed any more encouragement. Carly shot out of the vehicle quicker than any sniper's bullet. She made her way over to the damaged car with Nick right on her heels. Knowing it was useless to try to convince him to stay out of the open, she didn't bother. Instead, she focused on the backseat.

Empty.

Please, no, no, no...

Breaths came in quick spurts, fueled by her rising panic. She couldn't lose the children; she'd promised. Maria lay to the rear of the vehicle. Grady was slumped against the driver's door, pinned against the ground.

Mason hurried for Grady while Carly checked on Maria. Maria's pulse beat against her fingers in a steady rhythm, but the gash on her head didn't look good.

"Christopher! Lindsey!" Nick called their names, his voice hoarse, trembling with suppressed emotion. Her heart ached for him, pounded with adrenaline as she refused to think they wouldn't find them.

She looked at Mason as the ambulance pulled up along with several police cars. "Grady?"

Grimly, he shook his head. "He's alive, but it doesn't look good. He's trapped under the steering wheel. I'm not sure where all the blood is coming from. Looks like he's in shock, though."

Sorrow hit her. "Maria managed to climb out of the

vehicle as though she was going after the kids." Carly looked around and came to a decision. "Okay, you handle Grady and Maria. I'm going with Nick to look for the children."

"They're probably long gone from here, Carly."

She knew that. Didn't want to acknowledge it. Rescue workers surrounded the car while officers combed the wooded area. Maria and Grady were in good hands.

"Christopher!" She whirled at the shout and saw Nick grab the seven-year-old into his arms. Relief nearly brought her to her knees.

Carly raced over to the pair. "Where's Lindsey?"

Christopher had a stranglehold on his uncle, and she could hear the boy's wheezing. He also had several superficial cuts on his forehead and one on his cheek.

"Where's his inhaler?" she asked.

Christopher lifted his head. "Car. Backpack." He pointed. Carly sprinted back to the car and climbed through the rear window, shoving the shattered glass out of the way. She spotted the backpack and snatched it.

Up front, she saw that one of the paramedics had his fingers on Grady's neck while Mason looked on. She shot him a frantic look. The grim shake of his head didn't encourage her. But she didn't have time to think about that now.

Once out of the car, she rummaged in the side pocket of the backpack until her fingers closed over the device that would ease Christopher's asthma. Then she had to find the boy's sister.

Quickly, she made her way back to Christopher and pushed the inhaler into his hand. He placed it between his lips and pulled in two quick puffs. Almost immediately, color started seeping back into his cheeks.

"Where's Lindsey?" Nick repeated Carly's question.

"Back there," her brother said. "She's scared."

Nick planted a kiss on the boy's head, and Carly sprinted in the direction Christopher had indicated. The area he'd come from looked trampled, so she followed the path and almost stumbled over the body that lay in front of her.

Getting on her radio, she called for a paramedic, but knew it wouldn't do any good. The man had a bullet hole in his chest and one in his stomach. And that was just what she could see.

"Lindsey?" she called. "Where are you, honey? It's all right. You're safe now."

Nick's voice joined hers. "Lindsey?"

A whimper behind the bushes to the right of her pulled Carly in that direction. Nick shifted Christopher and tromped right after her. "Stay back," she told him in a hushed voice.

"No way."

"Look, Lindsey hasn't come out. Maybe there's a reason for that."

She wouldn't have thought it possible, but his face paled even more. "You think…"

"That someone has her and is keeping her from coming out? I don't know. Just let me check it out, will you? Keep Christopher at a safe distance."

Torn, indecision twisting his features, he finally nodded and backed up a few steps to shelter Christopher behind one of the other bushes.

But he kept his eyes trained on her.

Carly kept her gun ready, not knowing what lay beyond the bush in front of her. She just prayed no one on the other side sent a bullet through it. She had no protection. But she didn't have a choice: she had to get to Lindsey.

She could hear movement behind her and turned to see two other officers ready to come to her defense. She gave them a thumbs-up and they nodded their willingness to let her continue to take the lead.

With one hand clutching her weapon, she reached with the other to shift the bushes so she could see behind them.

What she saw made her gasp. She scanned the area and, seeing no immediate threat, holstered her gun. Turning to the officers behind her, she motioned for them to search the area. "Nick, come here."

Lindsey sat on the ground, knees pulled to her chest, forehead resting on them. She had her arms wrapped around her legs and was rocking back and forth, crying without making a sound.

"Oh, Lindsey." Carly dropped beside the girl, her throat swelling with unshed tears. "It's okay, darling. Can I put my arms around you?"

Still Lindsey didn't answer, just stayed in her tight little ball, rocking. Carly heard Nick come around the bush, Christopher still gripped in his arms. His breath left his lungs in a *whoosh*. He went to set the boy on the ground, but Christopher wouldn't let go of his neck. "Chris, I need to check on your sister."

"No." The child buried his face in Nick's neck.

Carly rested a hand on Lindsey's arm, and when the girl didn't shrug her off, she slid her hand along the back of her shoulders until she had an arm around her. Then, in one smooth move, Lindsey released her legs to wrap her arms around Carly's waist. Her sobs broke free, and Carly let her cry.

Heart breaking for the girl, she looked up at Nick. The furious expression on his face stunned her. Pure rage glittered down at her. In her heart she knew he was regretting his decision to place his children's safety in her hands.

She couldn't blame him. Guilt hammered at her.

She should have done something. Stopped all this from happening…somehow.

But how? Her mind raced. How?

She couldn't come up with an answer. And right now, they needed to get to the car and get somewhere safe. She pulled the girl to her feet just as Mason arrived, diverting her attention from Lindsey. She didn't release the girl, just motioned for everyone to walk toward the car.

Carly shot a look at Mason, who had his gun drawn and his eyes roaming their surroundings. "Maria? Grady?"

"Both are still alive. No one can tell us what happened here yet, though."

"I know what happened."

Christopher's outraged little voice made Carly blink. Mason looked at Nick then said, "Tell us when we get in the car, little guy."

But Christopher talked anyway. "The bad man shot the car bunches of times. Mr. Grady said a bad word, and then Ms. Maria told us to get down on the floor and pull our backpacks on top of our heads."

Lindsey's sobs had stopped. Now the girl shuddered, hiccupped and sniffed. Carly finally got a good look at her face. She, too, had some superficial wounds. A few looked like they may have come from tree branches. A bruise on her right cheek was already forming.

Christopher said, "Then the car rolled and hit something hard. I was really scared."

"I know you were, Chris, but you're doing great," Nick encouraged him. Reaching the car, Mason continued his surveillance as Nick, Carly and the kids slid inside.

"Then the bad man came up to the car, and Ms. Maria shot him and he fell down. Then me and Lindsey climbed out of the broken window in the back and ran into the woods to hide."

"Is that all?"

"No." His eyes teared up, and he balled up his little fists. "The bad man followed us even though he was bleeding a whole lot. He grabbed Lindsey, and she screamed. Then he put a gun near her head and said something to her, but he whispered it and I couldn't hear what he said. Then he coughed and walked funny. He even ran into a tree. But then he disappeared. Then you called my name, and I came to find you." He glared in the direction that the man he'd just described had gone. "I wish I had a gun. I'd a shot him for scaring Lindsey like that."

Carly watched Nick blink several times then swallow before he could speak. "You're a good brother, Chris. Thanks for telling us what happened. Now, let's get the paramedics to check you out, okay?"

Nick wanted to kill someone. With his bare hands. Then he felt guilty for the feeling. *God, I need You. I need Your calming presence, Your wisdom and the strength to do whatever it is You would have me do.*

He paced the floor of the safe house where they'd finally arrived two hours ago. The paramedics had declared the children relatively unharmed, other than a few bumps and bruises from being tossed around inside the car. But neither had hit their heads or claimed to have any pain. He'd watch them closely over the next few hours, and if anything developed, he'd get them to the nearest hospital. So far, other than being traumatized by the incident, they seemed fine physically.

Carly now walked the exterior perimeter while Mason plowed a path through the interior. The kids were finally asleep. Debbie had supper waiting for them when they arrived, and they filled her in on the details of the day.

Nick called Wayne Thomas, Debbie's father, and asked

him to take care of a few things since he was going to be out of commission for the next few days. Nick had a decision to make and needed to be able to think without worrying about the distraction of his job.

Wayne had blown out a sigh. "Nick, take this pressure off your shoulders. Let me have the case. I can rearrange my schedule and do this for you."

And for the first time in his life, Nick had seriously considered giving in. The vision of Lindsey's terrified huddle in the woods wouldn't leave him. She still hadn't said a word to anyone. And Christopher had had a hard time letting Nick go tonight.

"I...I... Let me think about it, Wayne. I don't want to do anything to put you in danger, either."

Wayne had laughed. "Look, Nick, you've got two small children to take care of. Debbie's a big girl and understands the situation. She can just move in with me and let the marshals do their job here. At least Christopher and Lindsey wouldn't be targets anymore. I'd hate to think what would happen if..."

"Yeah, yeah." Nick sighed. "Let me sleep on it tonight. Giving in to these people is wrong. So wrong I can't even..." He paced from one end of the room to the other. "But putting Chris and Lindsey through this isn't right, either. I'll get back to you."

"Sure, Nick. I got you."

Nick thanked God every day for the friendship he had with Wayne. Nick cleared his throat. "Talk to you soon."

He'd hung up then checked on the kids. Both had been asleep. Now he felt the need to check again. The back door opened and Carly came in, her brow furrowed, deep in thought.

Nick let her think. He couldn't talk to her at the moment.

She caught his eye before he could turn down the hallway. "Are you all right?"

"Yes. I'm just going to check on the kids."

He felt her eyes on his back all the way down the hall.

Christopher lay sacked out on his back, snoring gently, his breathing deep and even, thank goodness. No hint of the wheezing that had been there earlier. The grip on the stuffed dog he was never without seemed tighter than usual, but for the most part, Christopher looked peaceful, untroubled by nightmares.

Soft steps took him to the room next door. Lindsey lay curled in a fetal position, her arms wrapped around a pillow, clutching it to her stomach. In her sleep, she flinched and frowned.

Nick stepped closer and laid a hand on her arm. He bowed his head and whispered a prayer. "Lord, please place Your healing and peaceful touch on Lindsey. Give her rest. Chase the bad memories and thoughts from her mind." He kept his hand there and felt Lindsey give a small sigh and saw her brow smooth out.

"How do you do it?"

Nick jumped at the whisper behind him. Carly. He turned to look at her. "What do you mean?"

She had her eyes on Lindsey's more peaceful form. "How do you keep your faith in the midst of all of this? Why do you keep turning to a God who seems to have His back to you?"

He walked toward her and placed a hand on her arm. The little ripple of awareness that surged through him caught him off guard. But he had to admit, he liked it.

And that set off even more ripples. Ripples of a different sort. Warning signals that said, "Watch out, this woman could be a danger to your heart." Clearing his throat, he said, "Let's go into the den."

She turned and led the way. While Debbie packed up the leftovers from supper, Mason sat at the kitchen table working on the laptop, searching for information on the man who'd been killed this afternoon. Nick walked into the kitchen and said, "Thanks for supper, Debbie."

The young woman smiled and gave a half-hearted chuckle. "No problem. What else am I going to do with my time? I guess I could have taken off for Europe or gone with Mr. and Mrs. Jefferson, but..." She shrugged. "I don't want to bail on the kids." She rubbed her hands together, and Nick clasped them between his.

She'd been there when his niece and nephew needed someone the most. She and her father. He gave her a gentle push toward the hall. "Get some rest, Deb. I'll listen for the kids tonight." He wouldn't be surprised if one of them had a nightmare.

Debbie smiled and raised up on her tiptoes to kiss his cheek. "Sure, Nick. Good night."

A ringing phone shattered the quiet, and Debbie gasped. Fishing in the pocket of her jeans, she pulled it out. Carly snatched it from her and clicked it off, then pulled the battery from it.

She and Mason exchanged looks.

"What?" The poor woman looked scared stiff. "I...I saw the number. It was my dad."

"You can't have your own cell phone here. We can get you an encrypted one, but until then, this one has to stay dismantled." Carly slid the phone into the kitchen drawer to her left. "I hope you understand."

Concern stamped on her pretty face, Debbie nodded. "Yes, that's fine." The frown lingered, and she looked like she wanted to say something else.

"What is it?" Carly prompted.

"I just...I hate to admit it, but I felt safer with the phone.

I mean, what if I'm with the children and something happens?"

"That's why we're here, Debbie. You won't have a need for it."

"Well, it's just…"

"It's like a security blanket, huh?" Carly asked knowingly.

Debbie blushed. "Yes, exactly. Stupid, huh?"

"Not at all. I understand, but I still can't let you have it."

Debbie's lips tightened. Then she shrugged. "All right, that's fine, but could someone call my father to let him know we're okay? I'm sure he just wasn't thinking when he called my cell. And the fact that he got hung up on is going to scare him."

"I'll do it," Mason volunteered. "Or better yet. Here." He handed her his encrypted phone, and Debbie gave him a weak smile.

"I'll just go in the bedroom and bring this back to you when I'm done. I'm really sorry, Nick. You know I wouldn't do anything to put you or the children in danger."

She blinked back sudden tears, and Nick patted her arm. "Don't worry about it, Deb. You didn't know."

"Okay," she whispered. "Thanks."

Nick watched her leave and then turned to find Carly studying him, a funny look on her face. "What?"

"You don't have a clue, do you?"

"Clue?"

She bit her lip and shook her head. Turning to Mason, Carly asked, "Anything?"

Mason looked up from his task and shook his head. "Not yet. I'll find what I'm looking for, though."

Carly settled on the couch and looked around. The house plan was a simple one. Open and airy on the inside, nondescript on the outside. Situated on the outskirts of town on a little farm, the windows covered, shutting out the darkness of the night.

And any prying eyes.

Nick sat on the other end of the couch and leaned his head back against it. He stared at the ceiling, wishing he could just go to sleep and shut out the world. But since that wasn't an option, he waited for Carly to start.

It didn't take her long. "What is it, Nicholas?"

"You said I didn't have a clue. About what?"

"Debbie."

"Ah. Well, that's not totally true. I have a small clue."

"That she's completely in love with you?"

His lips curved in a rueful smile. "No, she's not."

"Nick…"

"It's not love. Infatuation, maybe. A little hero worship or something like that. But not love. She doesn't know what love is yet."

"And you do?"

A pause. "Yeah. I do." He shut his eyes. "Love is patient. Love is kind. It doesn't envy, it doesn't boast. It's not proud or rude or self-seeking or quick to anger. It doesn't keep track of wrongs…"

"Love does not delight in evil but rejoices with the truth. It always protects, always trusts, always hopes, always perseveres." Carly finished the quote.

Surprised, he looked at her. "You know your Bible."

"First Corinthians 13. I had to memorize it one year for camp. I've never forgotten it."

"I thought you didn't believe in God."

Carly sighed. "I believe in Him. I just don't understand Him. Don't even think I like Him very much."

"Why?"

Carly shifted, obviously uncomfortable with the turn

in the conversation. "I don't know. Maybe I've seen too much, become disillusioned. I don't understand why He lets things happen the way He does. Why the bad guys seem to win more than the good guys." She gave a self-deprecating smile and shrugged.

He raised his brows. "I have a feeling it's a lot more than that. But I know what you mean, and I understand where you're coming from. I've seen a lot on my end, too."

She studied him. "But it didn't happen to you."

"Oh, yes, it did." Was now the right time to explain? Would she hear him, really hear him?

Interest lifted a brow, and she leaned forward. "But you still have your faith. You still pray to a God who let you down."

Nick reached out and snagged the fingers that absently worked the fringe of one navy blue pillow. They stilled at his touch. "God didn't let me down. I just had to come to the realization that I'm not going to understand everything this side of heaven. Trying to understand the mind of God is exhausting. Trust me, I've been there." He intertwined his fingers with hers and studied her hand. Strong fingers with short, blunt-cut nails. Soft hands that could soothe with a touch....

Stop it, Nick, he ordered himself. Lifting his gaze to connect with hers, he saw the pink in her cheeks, and the longing in her eyes grabbed his heart. Longing for him? Or for the God she'd decided had let her down?

Not wanting to ask, he said, "But I do believe Him when He says He loves me. I believe He's who He says He is, but..." He looked away and swallowed hard. "I'll admit it's not always easy. Sometimes I really have to work at it. To remind myself of the times I've felt His presence, seen His hand working when I didn't understand the circumstances."

She drew in a deep breath and said, "I thought you'd be really mad at me after what happened today with the kids."

Her change of topic startled him. "Mad at you? Why?"

Her throat bobbed, and she spread her hands. "I didn't keep them safe. I saw the expression on your face at the scene of the accident... You were furious."

Blinking, he recalled the emotions going through him when he saw Lindsey in the woods. He squeezed her fingers. "No, Carly, I wasn't mad at you. I was mad at me."

She froze. "You were?"

"Yeah. Because I'd been so stubborn about moving to a safe house." Remembered fear shuddered through him. "I was the one who put my kids in jeopardy, not you."

"But I should have—"

"Carly, quit second-guessing yourself. You weren't anywhere near the children. There was nothing you could have done."

"I should have insisted—"

"Hey, Carly, Nick," Mason called from the kitchen. "I've got an identity on our dead guy in the woods. The captain at the police department just sent it to me. I've been reading his rap sheet for the last ten minutes."

Nicholas realized he still held her hand in his and let it go—reluctantly.

Carly jumped up, the flush on her cheeks speaking volumes. So, she wasn't unaffected by him. He didn't know whether he was glad or not. As she went to stand and look over Mason's shoulder at the computer, he couldn't help but heed the warning his heart continued to beat.

He followed her more slowly, pondering his feelings, his thoughts. Okay, he would admit he was attracted to her, but that didn't mean he had to act on those feelings.

Because whoever he became romantically involved with wouldn't just affect his heart. He now had two children to consider.

Two children who'd already lost two women they'd loved, a mother and an aunt. What happened if he and the children fell in love with Carly and she was killed, not necessarily even on the job? What if she had a car wreck or...?

Did he dare take a chance on loving and losing her?

Did he have a choice anymore?

Loving and losing hurt.

So did living too carefully and not to the fullest.

He was close enough to breathe in the fragrance that was completely her own. Longing stirred, not just for the physical intimacy marriage offered, but for the companionship, the security in knowing the person he loved returned his affection, a spiritual equal....

And there lay another problem. Carly's lack of faith. Until she came to terms with God—

"Nick? Hello? Anyone there?" came Carly's voice.

He blinked, then flushed. "Oh, sorry, I was thinking."

"About?"

"N-nothing." He'd almost said *you*, and her intense gaze told him she knew it. He tore his eyes away. "What do you have?"

Skepticism greeted his avoidance, but she didn't press him. "Do you recognize this man? Terrence Brown?"

He looked at the face on the screen and felt the familiar tug of recognition. "I've probably seen him in my courtroom at one point or another."

"He's the one who was killed today at the scene," Mason offered. "He's got known ties to de Lugo. Strong ties."

"Okay. Just more evidence to add to the man's already thick folder."

Mason sighed. "These guys mean business, Nicholas. We need to make sure every precaution is taken. Because I've got to tell you." He looked up and met Carly's gaze, then Nick's. "You don't want those kids falling into the hands of these people."

EIGHT

Carly swallowed hard. Mason's words punched her, bringing home the fact that they could have lost the children today.

Nick looked sick then covered the expression, hardening his jaw and balling his fingers into a fist. "I know. That's why I'm considering..."

He paused and looked away, swallowing hard.

Carly placed a hand on his arm, felt his muscles bunch under her fingers. Warmth immediately suffused her hand, and she snatched it away as discreetly as possible. Her cheeks felt hot, and she put some distance between herself and Nick. Mason had a bemused look on his face for a split second before he turned back to the computer.

Why was she feeling this way? What about Hank, her friend and mentor, who now lay in his grave because of this man? Somehow the argument had lost its punch. Getting to know Nick again, watching him with his children, had lessened the hurt in her heart. His faith had even made her long to find her way back to God.

Hank wouldn't blame Nick. He'd blame the man who pulled the trigger. And he still would have forgiven.

Drawing in a steadying breath, Carly asked, "What exactly are you considering?"

"Giving in."

Shock made her flinch as she stared at him for a moment. Then she asked, "What? Are you serious?"

Nicholas slapped the back of the chair and stalked to the kitchen bar. He placed his forearms on the counter and bowed his head. "Yes. I can't let the children continue to live this way—and I can't send them away. It's not right, and I have to put them first."

"No, you don't, Uncle Nick."

Carly snapped her head around to the door. Lindsey stood there, barefoot, hair spilling around her shoulders. Dark circles rimmed her eyes. She looked so small, defenseless. Nick raised a brow. "Eavesdropping again, Linds?"

Lindsey blushed. "Sorry."

Carly walked over to her and placed an arm around her thin shoulders. "Did we wake you, honey?"

"No." She gave a wry smile that looked surprisingly mature on her young face. "*You* didn't."

"Nightmares?" Sympathy tugged her.

"Yes."

Nick walked over and pulled the girl into a hug. She slipped her arms around his waist and closed her eyes. "You can't do it, Uncle Nick," she murmured against his chest.

Placing a finger under her chin, he lifted her head to look at him. "What do you mean? I thought you wanted me to pass the case to another judge."

A tear dripped from the corner of her eye to disappear into her hairline. "I did...until today."

Nick shot Carly a confused look. She shrugged, and he gazed back down at his niece. "Okay, you want to tell me why you've had a change of heart? I would have thought what happened today, the nightmares that just woke you, would have made you feel even stronger about it."

Lindsey pulled in a shuddering breath. "I was so scared, Uncle Nick. I can't even put it into words..."

Nick's jaw went rigid, and he trailed a hand down Lindsey's unblemished cheek to tuck a strand of hair behind her ear. "I know, darling. That's why—"

"No, wait, let me finish."

He nodded, and Carly inched closer. Lindsey heard her and turned to reach out and grasp Carly's hand. Surprised, Carly gave her a reassuring squeeze.

Lindsey said, "He put the gun up to my head." She released Carly's hand to touch her temple then slid her fingers back into Carly's palm. "He...he said to tell you that you would die and that everyone would die just like..." She bit her lip and another tear escaped.

Nick wiped it away and whispered, "Just like...?"

Carly tensed. She had a feeling she knew where this was going.

"Just like my mama," Lindsey finally whispered.

Nick just shut his eyes, struggling for control. Carly felt a mixture of emotions surge inside her. Hurt, anger, the desire to get back at the people doing this to this family she'd come to care about in such a short time.

Nick pulled back and grasped Lindsey's arms in his big hands. He looked straight into her eyes. "Linds, I've already decided to pass this case on to Debbie's father. I won't put you and Christopher in danger anymore."

Carly watched Lindsey's jaw harden in an exact imitation of her uncle. She looked so much like him at that moment, it was eerie. "No. You have to do this. It's just like you said before. If you let the bullies get away with bullying, it gives them power they shouldn't have, and they just keep on being bullies. And it makes you feel weak for giving it to them. I'll admit that guy scared me when he pointed that gun at me..." She swallowed hard again. "But it also made me mad, so mad I promised that if he didn't kill us, I'd make sure you didn't quit the case."

Shock rendered him speechless. When he found his voice, it was low. "Lindsey, hon, I—"

"I mean it, Uncle Nick." Her earnest face pressed closer to his. "You can't let them win. You have to put them in jail where they belong, or they'll go around doing this to other people. And that's just wrong."

He cleared his throat. "Yes. Yes, it is."

"So, you have to do this trial and trust that Ms. Carly and Mr. Mason and God will keep us safe, okay?"

Nick looked at Carly. When his eyes touched hers, she blinked, not even realizing she had tears swimming in them. One dripped down her cheek, and she gave it a quick swipe.

His gaze back on his niece, Nick raised a hand to rub his chin and blow out a sigh. "Lindsey...I don't know what to say."

"Say you'll do the trial and not give it to Mr. Wayne." She squeezed his hand. "When Mom died, you gave him a lot of cases, and some of the bad people went free, remember?"

"Some did, but I'm sure Mr. Wayne had good reasons. If I had handled those cases, I probably would have had to do the same thing. This is different. I can't stand to see you in danger. You're all I have left of your mom and..." Carly could see him struggling to control his emotions as he stood and breathed in deep.

Lindsey stepped forward and wrapped her arms back around her uncle's waist. "I know," she said into his chest, "and she would want you to make the world a safer place for me and Chris. You've got to do this. I really believe that now. And everything you've been preaching about doing what's right and not giving in to bullies makes sense." She looked up at him. "So you've got to do your job and make sure they don't get off on some technicality or whatever, okay?"

Nick squeezed her shoulders. "When did you get so smart?"

"When you don't think I'm listening to you."

Carly coughed to cover up a laugh. Nick smiled then sighed. "I'll think about it. Now go back to bed. It's late."

She gave him a little smile. "Well, it's not like I have to get up and go to school, right?"

He laughed again, and Carly joined in, appreciating the attempt to lighten the heavy mood. "Right. But go to bed anyway."

"Okay. 'Night."

Before she could turn away, Nick placed his hands under her arms and lifted her straight up to place a kiss on her cheek, then lowered her back to the floor.

She grinned, surprised and delighted. "You haven't done that since I was a kid."

"You still *are* a kid, Linds. Now scram."

With a giggle, Lindsey darted down the hall to her bedroom, her steps lighter. Carly was sure her heart was, too.

She looked at Nick. "Wow."

"Yeah. Out of the mouths of babes, huh?"

"I'll say. So…I guess you have a lot of thinking to do."

"A lot of praying."

"And that."

Carly's phone rang, and she snatched it from her belt. "Hello?"

"Hey," came a weak voice.

"Maria. How are you doing?"

"Better. I wanted to call. I figured you guys had some questions."

"Definitely. Do you mind if I put you on speakerphone?"

"No, that works."

Carly motioned for the guys to gather around the table and set her phone in the middle. "Okay, go ahead."

"I know you found the children. I'm so relieved—and so sorry this even happened."

Nick spoke up. "They're safe now. That's all that matters. That, and you and Grady getting better."

"Yeah, I hear Grady's not doing too well." Sadness thickened her voice. Then she cleared her throat. "Anyway, when we left the school, everything seemed to be fine, and then bullets started hitting the car from out of nowhere. The bulletproof glass couldn't hold up to whatever they were shooting."

"They came prepared with armor piercing .308 slugs," Mason said. "They put enough of them in the back windshield to finally shatter it. The bullet that hit Grady broke a rib, which pierced a lung. He was incredibly fortunate. In fact, I'd say it's amazing he survived."

"Oh, I didn't know what we'd been hit with. It felt like an explosion. How are the kids?"

"Some bumps and bruises, but okay overall," Carly said. "The back windshield held long enough for them to get on the floor. Thankfully, none of the bullets found them." Just the thought sent her stomach churning. The look on Nick's face said he felt the same. She switched gears. "Maria, Christopher was able to tell us a little about what happened, but can you fill us in on the rest of it?"

"What do you need?"

"After you shot the perp—whose name was Terrence by the way—Terrence Brown—what happened?"

"Um, I saw the kids run off into the woods. I'd told them to hide. Then I saw the perp running after them. I tried to follow them, but guess I passed out."

"Okay, that's basically what Christopher said."

"But Carly..." She paused. "How did they know which route we were taking? They had to have been waiting for us."

Carly froze. "Waiting for you? You mean they didn't follow you?"

"Um...no. No, they were waiting. Right when we passed, I remember a flash of something, then the bullets slamming into the back windshield."

"Then they had prior knowledge."

Her gaze shot to Mason, who nodded. "Yeah, I've already thought about that."

"So what did you come up with?"

"Nothing, really. They could have been watching the roads, anticipating that we'd take the kids out of school as soon as Nick got the call and saw the video."

Maria interrupted. "What video?"

Carly leaned in. "Nick got a call and a video of the kids. Then Lindsey entering the classroom. We could see her before you shut the blinds." She tried to keep her tone accusation-free, but wasn't entirely successful.

Silence greeted her. Then a heavy sigh filtered through. "Lindsey pushed through ahead of me. I told her to wait in the hall, but she ignored me. By the time I got through the crowd, she was already in the classroom."

Carly sat back with a sigh and looked at Nicholas. "All right. Well, things have changed since then. Lindsey's cooled it with the attitude and seems to understand the seriousness of the situation now."

"Good." Relief sounded in Maria's voice, and Nick

nodded in agreement. "I'm just glad she realized it before something—"

"Thanks for filling us in on the situation at the school," Nick interrupted. He looked at Carly. "I think we can just keep this to ourselves. I'd talk to Lindsey about it if she hadn't come in earlier, but now..."

"I agree."

A sound came from the other end of the line. Then Maria said, "I've got to go. Keep me posted."

"Take care of yourself, Maria." Carly hung up and rubbed her eyes.

"I'm all hyped up on caffeine," Mason said. "Why don't you guys try to get some rest? I'm sure tomorrow's going to bring its own brand of excitement."

Carly stood. "Great. I'll take you up on that. Wake me in four hours." She looked at Nicholas and said, "If you have earplugs, you might want to put them in before you go to bed. You might not remember from two years ago, but Mason snores."

"Hey!" Mason looked offended. "I do not."

With a roll of her eyes and a pointed look at Nicholas, she headed down the hall to the room she'd share with Lindsey. Christopher, Nicholas and Mason would share another room. And Debbie had the third bedroom. She wondered if any of the adults would really get much rest. For more reasons than what happened earlier today.

However, she knew if she didn't force herself to sleep, she would lose her edge. And she couldn't afford that. So she slipped out of her shoes, shoved her gun under her pillow and closed her eyes.

Even as she drifted off, her brain worked over the problems the day had presented. One: How had the caller gotten Nick's private cell phone number? Two: How had the shooters known which route Maria and Grady were going to take? Three: Why hadn't the shooter killed Lindsey when he'd had the chance? Or had he even really had a chance? Four: How was Carly going to keep her heart out of this assignment when she couldn't deny the intense attraction she felt for Judge Nicholas Floyd?

It was going to be a long four hours.

NINE

Carly sipped her coffee and watched the sun come up through the slight crack in the blinds. Cracked just enough for her to see out, but no one to see in.

Surprisingly, the night had been quiet, and she'd slept soundly for the duration of her allotted time. Exhaustion hadn't given her a choice, and she'd forced herself not to think about what could happen while she slept. She knew Mason was on duty and would wake her should the need arise.

He'd given her five hours, and she was grateful. She'd done the same for him before. No doubt he'd read her like a book, noting that her fatigue went deeper than the physical. She'd needed the rest to recharge mentally, emotionally.

Now she contemplated how best to keep the family safe. She could hear Mason's snoring from her perch in the kitchen. He still didn't believe her when she said he sounded like a freight train.

Movement to her right made her start. She turned to see Debbie pad into the kitchen and head for the coffeemaker. "Good morning," Carly said.

"'Morning," Debbie mumbled. She grabbed her mug, made her way to the table and set it down with a thunk.

She sank into the chair and looked at Carly with bleary eyes. "I need earplugs."

Carly fought a grin but didn't think she was very successful. "I know. You get used to it after a while."

"Never. I pity the woman who marries him."

A laugh escaped this time, and Carly secretly agreed. "I guess I don't have to ask how you slept."

More footsteps sounded. Nick. Looking rumpled, grumpy, sleepy—and very, very attractive in his sweats and muscle T-shirt.

"Good morning, Nick." Tongue in cheek, she asked, "So, how'd you sleep?"

He glared at her. "You need a new partner—or I need a new roommate."

This time she giggled. She couldn't help it. "I warned you. Earplugs help."

"That man sounds like Joshua's pet pig, Uncle Nick," Christopher declared as he scooted up to the table. "What stinks?" He coughed, then declared, "I want pancakes."

Nick's lips curved. His eyes met Carly's, and she had to look away. He looked so appealing, so powerful, so... male.

He's a job, Carly. Stay focused on keeping him safe, not thinking about kissing him. But it was hard, because the more she was around him, the more she liked him. And the children.

She felt her lips curl in a smile. She knew for a fact he didn't snore. Then she frowned. Or Mason's snores had drowned his out.

Huh.

Then her lips turned south. *What are you thinking, Carly? You have no right to consider a relationship with him, no matter how much the idea appeals to you—at least not until the trial is over. If he was interested.*

But he was. She could see it in his eyes. But she could also see something that held him back, kept him from getting too close—even though he wanted to. There was a distance there that she couldn't explain. Maybe that was for the best. For now. She still wasn't sure she'd resolved the issue of Hank's death by a murderer Nick had released only hours before the murder.

Just the thought of that sent all romantic feelings skidding to the side. Sniffling, she decided Christopher was right. Something did smell. She frowned. What was it?

Her mind set off alarm signals, but she wasn't sure where the threat was coming from.

Nicholas examined the contents of the cabinet and turned to Christopher. "You're in luck. We've got the makings for pancakes."

Debbie stood. "Oh, I'll do that, Nick."

He smiled. "Thanks, but I've got it."

For a moment, she looked unsure, then shrugged. "Fine. I'll go check on Lindsey."

Carly stood, and her head spun. A wave of nausea hit her, and she gasped.

Nick caught her arm. "Are you all right?"

Pulling away, she grimaced. "Yes, I think so. I'm just going to take a look around outside."

Christopher coughed again, and Carly shot a sharp look at him. "Is he all right?"

Frowning, Nick studied his nephew. "I'll keep an eye on him." Without taking his eyes from Chris, he said, "After I finish the pancakes, I'm going to do some work. Is there an Internet connection here?"

"Yes, and it's encrypted, so you should be all right."

Still feeling slightly ill and wondering what that odor was, Carly headed for the door while Nick pulled out the frying pan then turned toward the refrigerator.

Outside, the muggy heat hit her. Silence enveloped her in the early morning. Oppressive silence.

A disconcerting quiet that just didn't seem natural.

She pulled in a deep breath and immediately felt better. The nausea stopped, and the dizziness faded.

However, her nerves tightened and the hair stood up on the back of her neck. She'd just walked out the door and no birds sang, no early morning crickets chirped.

Nothing.

"Something's not right," she whispered. But what?

No one was out there. No one knew where they were, and no one could be watching. Could they?

Keeping her expression neutral, her actions unhurried in case she was being watched, she turned and stepped back inside.

A spurt of laughter then a long breathless cough from Christopher greeted her. Debbie, looking wan and sleep-deprived, sat at the table making funny faces at the boy. Lindsey had yet to put in an appearance.

Nick turned from mixing the pancake batter, the smile on his lips sliding off as he sent a worried look at Christopher. Then he caught Carly's expression. Immediately, his eyes narrowed and his shoulders tensed. Voice low, he asked, "What is it?"

Not wanting to be an alarmist, yet knowing enough to listen to that inner voice that had saved her life more than once, she said, "I'm not sure, but I think everyone needs to get ready to move again."

"They found us?"

"Like I said, I'm not sure yet. Let me get Mason."

"I'm here." His voice came from the doorway. "What is it?"

Lindsey stumbled into the kitchen. "Uncle Nick? I don't feel so good."

"I feel kind of sick myself." Debbie put her hands on her head.

Christopher yawned. "My head hurts. Why am I so sleepy again? It hurts to breathe."

Carly noticed the headache starting behind her eyes. Outside, she'd felt fine. Inside...

She looked at the stove. Nick's hand reached to start the gas burner, and fear hit her. Carly yelled, "No! Don't touch that! Get Christopher and his inhaler. We all need to get out into the fresh air."

He jerked back and stared at her.

"There's a gas leak somewhere. That's the smell. We need to get out."

Mason stood and grabbed the keys. "They can't go outside. They'll be exposed. Everybody head toward the garage and get in the car."

Nick raced toward the bedrooms. "I'll get our stuff."

Carly tried to stop him. "Leave it. Just get out."

His gave her a sharp look. "You're planning on grabbing stuff. I'm not leaving you in here to do that alone." He looked at Debbie. "Get the kids and go, quickly."

She looked down at her sweats. Nick read her mind. "Don't worry about changing. You need fresh air."

Debbie nodded, raced to grab a few items from the kitchen counter. Carly almost yelled at her that they weren't important, but decided not to argue. Arguing took time, and one of the items was Christopher's stuffed dog. He'd need the comfort it provided.

In seconds, she'd gathered what meager belongings they needed and met Nicholas in the hallway. Debbie had already ushered the kids out to the car. "We need to go, now."

"I need my laptop and Chris's inhaler, and we're out of here."

He snatched the computer off the table, cord and all, and together they headed for the door. Carly picked up the inhaler from the kitchen counter, vaguely wondering why Debbie hadn't grabbed it.

Nausea swirled in the pit of her stomach once again. Her head ached, and her throat felt scratchy. Nick looked like he didn't feel so great, either. "As soon as we get into some fresh air, we'll feel better."

"Gas poisoning?"

"I suspect."

"On purpose, or a badly timed accident?"

"Good question. We'll treat it as a crime scene until proven differently." She exited the back door, stepping into the garage. She saw everyone already piled in the SUV, kids in the back and Debbie in one of the captain's chairs in the middle, Mason at the wheel.

Carly climbed in the front, and Nick sat behind her. Mason hit the button to activate the garage door. When he backed out, Carly took a deep breath of the fresh air and snatched her phone. Already the headache was receding and the nausea had calmed down. A glance in the rearview mirror showed everyone else had perked up, too.

"I didn't want to take a chance on using my cell phone in the house. I didn't know if it would be safe or not," Mason said. "But give me a minute to call this in."

Carly said, "I'll do it."

She punched in the number and leaned her head back to give a sigh of relief mixed with frustration. Relief they'd made it out without incident.

Frustration because it seemed like the de Lugos were able to stay one step ahead of them. It was like they had access to everything they were thinking.

Like they had inside information.

A chill seeped into her as she stared at the passing

scenery. While her mind processed that thought, her eyes automatically took in the details around and behind them.

Inside information.

Could it be possible?

But who?

The list of people who knew their whereabouts was very small. However, it must contain one person too many, and that person was doing his or her best to make sure Nicholas didn't make it to trial in three days.

Her boss, Chief Deputy U.S. Marshal Perry Chism, answered on the third ring. "Sir, we've got a problem." Explaining the situation didn't take long. Then she contacted the captain of the police department and filled him in. A team would be sent to the safe house to process it as a crime scene.

Carly said, "Oh, I put a cell phone in the far left drawer in the kitchen by the stove. Be sure to get that—I need to return it when this is all over." She looked at Nick. "Is there anything else they need to pick up?"

"I left one of Christopher's inhalers in the medicine cabinet in the bathroom."

She passed the information on to the captain, who promised to retrieve the items.

Tuning back in to the conversation between Mason and Nick, she vowed to sit down with the two men and try to figure out who could possibly be the one on the de Lugo payroll.

"Where are we going?" Christopher's little voice pierced the tense silence after Mason hung up. Carly turned to look at him. He'd taken a puff on the inhaler and already looked better.

Before she could answer him, Nicholas reached back

and took hold of his small hand. "We're headed for another safe house, little guy." He looked at Carly. "Am I right?"

She tried to paste a reassuring smile on her lips. "You got it in one." Speaking to Christopher, she said, "You have a very smart uncle."

This brought a long sigh, and, in all seriousness, Chris said, "I know. He must be, cuz he says I think just like him."

Carly choked on a laugh. She watched the stress on Nick's face dissolve into laugh lines and humor. Even Lindsey smiled. Debbie gave a brief chuckle then closed her eyes and leaned her head against the seat rest before popping back up. "I left the inhaler on the counter!"

"I got it," Carly reassured her.

"Oh, good."

Nicholas squeezed his nephew's hand then turned back around to face the front. When his eyes met Carly's, she saw the laughter had faded to worry. His brow furrowed, and that muscle jumped along his jaw. His look said they needed to talk. And soon.

She gave a short nod. She needed to talk to him, too. They needed to compile a list of people who'd known about the safe house and figure out who'd compromised it.

Carly felt the muscles along her jaw and neck tighten. It was hard enough trying to keep someone safe when you thought you knew who the good guys were. But when one of them crossed over...

The results were often deadly.

TEN

At the end of the long, winding, dirt road sat a one-story ranch-style house. Set apart from other houses on several acres of land, there were very few trees and nothing else in the vicinity that would make a good hiding place.

No one could get near the house without being exposed. A good safety measure and landscaped that way on purpose, Nick was sure.

As he watched the house come into view, he debated whether or not they were doing the right thing. It galled him that he'd tucked his tail and run, depending on the marshals to keep him safe, putting the responsibilities at his office off on someone else.

And yet, what choice did he have? Lindsey's terrified huddle in the woods wouldn't leave him. Christopher's clinging and fear-induced wheezing haunted him.

Bottom line: he had to protect the children.

And if staying in a safe house meant giving them peace of mind, then—

Mason interrupted his thoughts. "We're here."

He pulled into the garage and closed them in. Carly said, "Everyone stay in the car. I want to have a look around before we unload."

Shoulders stiff, Nick watched her climb from the car and,

with gun drawn, enter the house via the closest door. He looked at Mason. "Does she know something we don't?"

The man kept his eyes glued to the door Carly had just entered. "Nope, don't think so. She's just being extra careful." Mason met Nick's eyes. "It's a good thing."

Nick leaned back. He didn't like it. This feeling of helplessness. Watching someone he cared about—and he knew he was caring more every day—possibly walk into danger while he sat in the car. He reached for the door handle and shoved it open. "Well, I'm not sitting here while she's in there."

"That's her job, Nick. Just sit back and let her do it."

The words hit him between the eyes.

It was her job.

One she did every day.

A dangerous job that came with risk and the real possibility of dying.

When he'd gone through the police-academy training, it had been drummed into them how dangerous the job was and how important it was to watch your back constantly. He'd done as instructed, taken precautions and hadn't really worried about himself. But Carly...

Yep. He cared about her. A lot. Amazing how that had happened in such a short amount of time. But he couldn't deny the attraction he felt, the almost magnetic pull she had on him. At first he'd wondered if there was something more than partnership between her and Mason, but he'd quickly realized that they were good friends and nothing more.

He had felt glad, relieved.

That same relief flowed through him now. He realized he was glad Carly was the one who'd been chosen for this assignment. Glad she was with him. Originally, he hadn't wanted her on the assignment simply because he'd been a bit embarrassed. They'd shared some deep conversations two years ago and then hadn't seen each other since. It hadn't taken him long to realize that those conversations had laid a foundation that made it easier to care about her that much more now.

Watching her in action this time gave him a new respect for her and her abilities. Something to keep in mind when he considered the future. And if they made it out of this alive, a future with Carly was something he wanted to think about.

Seriously.

Less than three minutes later, Carly reappeared in the doorway and waved them in. "The back of the house looks good. There aren't any real windows in the back. I'm impressed. You have to look really close to realize it. Plantation shutters all around, so that keeps you from feeling boxed in. There's no way anyone can see in, so you can probably move around pretty freely back there. The front is a different story. A few windows that will have to be avoided, but we can do that."

"What about if we need a safe place in a hurry?" Mason asked.

"There's a covered walkway to an outbuilding. We've got an emergency vehicle in the other garage if we need it. The keys are in it, so we can use whichever one is closest at the time of trouble—if there is trouble."

"Hopefully, there won't be any more problems."

Nick decided he wouldn't hold his breath on that one. With a sigh, he climbed out and helped Debbie and the children out of the vehicle.

Grabbing the bags, he trailed them into the house. Another house that wasn't his own.

After determining the sleeping arrangements, the adults

convened in the living area and set it up to serve as a headquarters.

Carly paced while Nicholas set up his laptop. Mason talked on the phone with his superior, and the kids acquainted themselves with the layout of the house. Debbie checked out the pantry and appliances.

At the stove, she turned with a raised brow. "Well, at least this one is electric."

Carly gave her a smile, and Nicholas appreciated the attempt at humor. Carly nodded. "I'm just glad the gas company started adding that additive into the gas. Otherwise we probably wouldn't have known what hit us."

Nick rubbed the back of his head and caught Carly's eye. She stopped her pacing and stared at him. "What?"

"What if we went back to my house?"

"Excuse me?"

"Seriously. That would be the last thing they'd expect us to do, wouldn't it?"

Placing her hands on her hips, she seemed to consider it, then said, "They probably have someone watching the house. As soon as we pulled in the drive, word would be out." She paused. "And even if we sent someone to sweep the area, it would just alert them that something was up and you were possibly coming back."

Nick blew out a sigh. "All right, I guess that makes sense."

"Why don't you sit down and write down everyone you can think of that might have access to your whereabouts. I'll do the same, and we'll compare lists."

"Sounds like a plan."

Carly rounded up some paper, and while Debbie entertained the children, Nick and Carly got busy.

After thirty minutes, Nick slapped his pen down. Carly jumped. "What?"

"I can't think of anyone else."

She leaned forward, and the scent of peppermint drifted his way. He took in a deeper breath and savored the moment.

"Nick? You okay?" Looking into her eyes, he just studied her. She gave a nervous little laugh and said, "Hello?"

A slow smile crept across his lips, and in a voice for her ears only, he said, "You always smell so good. How do you do that?"

She blinked. Opened her mouth. Shut it.

He'd caught her by surprise. Well, he'd taken himself by surprise, too. He couldn't believe he'd let those words pass his lips.

But he had.

She became flustered. It warmed his heart to see her so unsettled. Not in a way that made him want to laugh at her, but in a way that encouraged him, emboldened him.

"Uh…well, I'm g-glad you like it," she stuttered.

"I do." He nodded, his voice sounding husky to his own ears. Clearing his throat, he said, "I like you, Carly."

He wouldn't have thought it possible, but her face turned an even darker shade of red.

She popped up out of her chair to pace to the other end of the kitchen. Leaning against the stove, she crossed her arms. "What are you doing, Nicholas?"

He followed her lead and stood, too. "What do you mean?"

"Why are you flirting with me?"

For a moment, he didn't answer then decided to shoot straight with her. "Because you intrigue me. I've never met anyone like you before, and I'm not sure exactly how to handle that. How to handle you—and my attraction to you. I keep wondering what it would be like to kiss you, and then I think about your job and how dangerous it is…."

He breathed in. "And then I'm back to thinking about kissing you. You're making me crazy—uh...in a good way. I think."

She drew in a deep breath then let it out. "Oh."

He waited. When she didn't say anything else, he asked, "That's it? 'Oh'?"

From the corner of her eye, she watched him, then smiled mysteriously. "Yeah. Oh." She pulled his piece of paper in front of her and said, "Now, what do you have?"

So that's how it was going to be. Did he let her get away with it? Or push it?

"Carly? Am I seriously out of practice or just plain crazy, because I think you feel the same attraction for me that I feel for you. Do you?"

She didn't answer for a minute. Then she looked him in the eye. "You're not crazy."

Joy flared in him. "Good, because—"

She held up a hand. "And that's all I'm going to say, because I have a job to do and I can't do that if I'm thinking about..." She waved a hand in the air and flushed. "You know...you thinking about me...in a way, that way...um... you know."

Then she ducked her head and went back to her list.

He got the message. Subject closed.

For now.

Carly looked at the short list in front of her. "Wayne Thomas, your secretary, the marshals. That's it?"

"That's it."

She grimaced. "Well, mine's not much better." She handed it to him. "I've got my boss, Grady and Maria." Then she frowned. "Wait a minute. Wayne Thomas? He knows where we are?"

"Sure. He'd be worried sick if he couldn't get in touch with Debbie."

"Okay, I want background checks done on everyone."

"Who is everyone?"

"Every person involved in this. People who know you, who have intimate knowledge of this trial and everything going on with it."

Mason came into the kitchen to look at the lists, then rubbed his chin. "We can do that. Let me see what I can do on the computer. Give me some names."

She hesitated, almost sick at the thought of what she was about to suggest. Nick stared at her. "Who?"

"Grady Fry and Maria Delucci."

Mason's jaw dropped. "Are you serious?"

"I don't want to be, but stranger things have happened in this business where money has a dangerous pull."

Her partner shook his head and crossed his arms. "I'm not doing background checks on fellow officers."

Carly stood. "Look, I don't necessarily suspect them, but we've got to cover all our bases. That means starting with the people closest to us."

"Then I suppose you want me to do one on each of us?" Mason quirked a brow at her, the redness in his cheeks telling her he wasn't happy at all with her suggestion.

Lifting her chin, she placed her hands on her hips. "Of course."

His shoulders relaxed a fraction, and he gave her a small smile. "Fine."

Mason looked at Nick. "We'll have to investigate Wayne and Debbie Thomas, too."

Carly froze, and she stared at her partner. "You're absolutely right." Her gaze shot to Nick. "Didn't you do one on her when you hired her?"

"No, of course not." He punched a clenched fist into

his other hand then raked that hand through his already tousled hair. She tried to ignore the way it just made him more appealing. A little ruffled, a lot rugged. His attractiveness constantly seared her. She blinked and honed in on his defense.

"She's Wayne's daughter. I trust her with my life."

"What about the lives of your niece and nephew?" she blurted.

That stopped him; the indignation on behalf of his friends receded. He let out a defeated sigh and hung his head. "I think it's ridiculous, but I guess we can't take the chance, can we?"

"I'd say not. We've got to nail this down." A cold sweat broke out across her upper body. "As of right now we don't trust anyone, okay?"

Nick covered her hand with his and squeezed. "Don't worry, Carly. We'll figure it out."

How did such a simple touch from Nick send awareness pinging through her nerves, making her hair feel like it must be standing on end? It just didn't seem possible. And yet it was. She felt it.

And if the look on his face meant anything, Nick did, too.

Mason beat an amused retreat back to his laptop in the den, and Carly took a deep breath. "Okay, so, any more ideas? Names?"

He spread his hands. "No. Unfortunately."

"Mason?" she called. "What about you?"

"I'm sending the requests for all the background checks. I don't like it, but I think you may be on to something."

"How long will it take to get a response?"

"Not too long."

A knock at the door sounded, and Carly nearly fell out of her chair. She shot to her feet and palmed her weapon.

Mason followed suit and said, "Nick, stay here. I'm going to get Debbie and the kids where I can see them. If this is a trap, I don't want anyone in the back of the house. Make sure you stay away from any windows."

Grim-faced, Nick did as requested while Carly planted herself on the side of the door. She called out, "Who is it?"

"It's Sandy Kessler from down the road a piece. I saw you drive up earlier and thought I'd welcome you to the neighborhood. Plus, I have a package for you. Someone dropped it off at my address by mistake. Happens all the time around here."

"Just a minute," Carly called out, buying Mason time to get the kids situated.

He appeared with the children in tow. Christopher clung to Debbie's hand while Lindsey's expression wavered between scared and mad.

"Get in the kitchen behind the island," Carly ordered. "It's the safest place for now."

The three hurried to do her bidding, and she waited for Mason to place himself opposite her. "Ready?" she mouthed.

He nodded.

Nick appeared back in her line of sight. He had his gun drawn and ready. She motioned him back, and he stepped into the doorway of the hall bath.

"A package?" Mason mouthed back. Carly's heart thudded. They'd just arrived two hours ago. No one should be sending them packages. Especially with this address on it. A safe house that only a handful of people knew about.

Apparently someone in that handful was one person too many.

Decision made, Carly holstered her gun and looked at Mason to whisper, "I'm going to answer the door. If I say I'm sick or something, she'll probably come back with a batch of chicken soup."

Mason nodded.

Peeling back the curtain from the window next to the door, Carly looked out and spied a short elderly woman standing there, gnarled, arthritic hands clutching a small box. Carly scanned the area behind and noted it was clear except for the small red Ford Taurus sitting at the top of the circular drive. From where she stood, the car looked to be empty, but Carly wasn't taking any chances. Someone could be lying down in the backseat ready to pop up and start shooting as soon as the opportunity presented itself.

Carly opened the door, caution making her movements slow. She kept one eye on the car and one on the woman's hands.

The woman smiled. "Hello. I'm Sandy."

Stepping from behind the door, Carly put on her welcome face. "Hello, Mrs. Kessler. I'm Carly." She left off her last name on purpose. "So nice to meet you."

"Like I said, I live about a quarter of a mile up the road. I saw you drive up a little while ago and wanted to make you feel welcome. Plus, I wanted to bring this to you. It has this address on it. Someone just rang my bell and left it a few minutes ago." She lifted the box toward Carly, who resisted the urge to step back. If it was going to explode, it would have done so when the woman handled it.

Unless it could be detonated by remote when the sender saw that the person he was after had it in his or her possession.

Hiding her trepidation, she took the package in one hand and smiled. "Thank you very much. That was very kind of you."

"Just being neighborly."

At the expectant look on her face, Carly thought fast. "I'd love to invite you in, Mrs. Kessler, but now just isn't a good time. Maybe after I get settled in a bit?"

"Oh, of course, dear. I understand."

"Uh, but where do you live exactly? I might like to visit sometime." Actually, she wanted to check out the woman's address and find out if anyone had seen the package being delivered.

Delighted, Mrs. Kessler recited the simple directions, and Carly promised to write them down as soon as she closed the door.

Once the little lady had driven off in her car, Carly shut the door and very gently laid the package on the kitchen table.

"What is it, Uncle Nick?"

The question came from Lindsey, who'd popped up from behind the kitchen island as soon as the door shut.

Nicholas glanced at his niece. "Not sure yet, honey, but I'm getting ready to find out." He looked at Debbie. "Why don't you and Christopher go with Debbie to the safe area while we figure out what's going on?"

Carly cleared her throat. "No way, Nick. You're going with them. There's no telling what's in that package." She studied it then drew in a deep breath. "All right, I'm guessing it's not a bomb or it would have gone off by now."

Mason shook his head. "It's not a bomb. They wanted her to deliver it to make sure we got it."

"Whose name is on it?"

Nick leaned over and read, "Judge Nicholas Floyd."

Carly didn't think it was a bomb, but she still had a really bad feeling about it. "Still, we can't take any chances. We need to get everyone out of the house and call for help. I don't want to touch that thing without backup."

Mason nodded. "I don't, either. Everyone into the safe area."

Nick shook his head. "It's not going to kill us," he said slowly, thoughtfully. "It's a power play."

Carly lifted a brow at his sudden statement. "What do you mean? So far they've tried to break into your house, snatch the children, kill you with poisonous snakes and possibly gas you or blow up the house if you sparked it." Exasperated, she looked at him. "What makes you think this is just some harmless little warning?"

"Because they can't get to me." In spite of the seriousness of the situation, his eyes warmed. "You're doing too good a job, and they can't put their hands on me—or the kids."

"But they seem to know where you are at all times. I really don't like that."

A frown flickered across his face. "Well, yes, there is that. But like I said, they're having trouble physically getting to me, and the trial starts the day after tomorrow. I'm betting this is where the mental anguish is supposed to come into play."

"Mental anguish?"

"Come on, Carly, I've studied the human mind and dealt with enough lowlifes in my career that I think I've gotten the hang of reading them pretty well. Let me open the box."

Carly sent him a hard-eyed stare. "Not a chance."

Mason hung up his phone and said, "I've just called for backup. We need to leave again. Obviously, they know you're here."

Nick shook his head. "No, someone's keeping them informed of every move we make." Grief cut into him as he considered what that meant. "It doesn't matter where we go. Someone close to me is an informant, someone I'd never suspect." He swallowed hard. "And that scares me." He glanced in the direction of the safe area. "A lot."

ELEVEN

Mason looked up from his phone. "Backup will be here in less than a minute. I'll be with the kids in the safe area. Send an officer to replace me as soon as one gets here."

Carly nodded, and Mason left.

Nick's fingers itched to open that deceptively innocent-looking package; however, he knew they were right. He couldn't take the chance of something deadly happening when the box was opened.

Thirty seconds later, three unmarked cars pulled into the drive and Carly greeted the four men and two women who entered the house.

Nick looked at Carly. "Debbie and the kids are in the safe area."

"Where?" an officer who looked to be about twenty-five and gave his name as Ben asked. Carly told him. "Stay with them until we give you the all clear, okay? Send Mason back in here with us."

"You got it."

He headed out to find them, and Carly watched a team of specialists take over the care of the package. She looked at Nick and opened her mouth. Before she could get the words out, he shook his head. "I'm not leaving."

He could tell she was exasperated, but he hadn't gone

to the police academy because he wanted to hide behind somebody's back. The only reason he'd agreed to the marshals' protection in the first place was because of the children.

This was about him, and he wasn't leaving.

A technician X-rayed the package and looked up. "It's not a bomb."

Nick felt a surge of triumph—and relief—that he'd been right.

"So, what's in it?" Nick demanded.

"Almost there," the technician said. He took the paper off, revealing a small brown box that looked like it could be purchased anywhere.

"Nick, you shouldn't be in here," Carly said. "You shouldn't even be in the same building as this thing."

"I'm staying." He could almost hear her molars grinding at his stubborn insistence. He looked at her. "This has to end now. We need to know who the inside person is."

Mason had returned from the safe area and gone back to his computer. "Whoa."

Nick saw him blanch at something on the screen. "What is it?"

"Did you know Debbie used to date a man associated with de Lugo?"

Everything inside Nick froze. "What? No, that's not possible."

"I just got the background checks back. Apparently, she was with him when he was arrested three years ago. She was released, and nothing ever went to trial because the charges were dropped."

"Then what's the big deal? It's probably just a coincidence. I know Debbie. She might have dated him, but she wouldn't have been involved in anything he was. Besides, she obviously hasn't had anything to do with him since then."

Mason's jaw firmed. "That you know of. I don't think I'd want to risk my kids' lives on that."

Nick felt sick.

Then the technician working on the box called out, "Hey, you guys want to see this?"

Nick spun around and strode to the man's side. Carly and Mason were right beside him. Looking into the box, he felt his heart stop.

A crushed inhaler just like the one used by Christopher lay on a bed of satin—the kind of material used in coffins. Carly drew in a deep breath, and Mason muttered a word Nick had never heard him use before.

His knees went weak. Then he shoved his way through the people in the den and headed for the secured area where the kids were.

He was right about the mental anguish. He honestly didn't know how much longer he could hold on before they cracked him. The trial started the day after tomorrow. Once he began presiding, the de Lugo family would have even more reason to get rid of him. They'd want to make sure he didn't finish the trial.

His resolve hardened. He'd send the children away. He had no choice. Then he'd move home and prepare for whatever the de Lugos threw at him.

Crossing the covered walkway, he ducked into the building.

And screeched to a halt. The carpeted area held a bowl of grapes, and the television played softly in the corner.

But the rest of the room was empty.

Footsteps sounded behind him. Carly nearly careened into his back. "Nick, are they okay?"

"They're not here."

Stepping farther into the room, she took in the vacant space. "But…but that's impossible. We sent someone back here to watch them."

"Let's check the garage."

She raced ahead of him and shoved the door open. "Oh, no. Lindsey! Chris!"

"Not again," Nick groaned, agony shooting through him.

The car was gone.

And so were the kids, Debbie and the officer she'd sent back here to watch out for them.

Carly got on her radio. "Mason, the car in the garage is gone. Get someone in here now. The kids are missing again."

Something glistened under the single bulb, and Nick stepped toward it. He bent down on one knee to examine the small drop of fluid. "Oh please, Lord, don't let that be—"

"Blood?" Carly whispered and squatted beside him. "I think it is." She grabbed an old towel from the bench beside her and dipped a corner into the liquid. She lifted it to her nose and sniffed. "That's definitely blood." She placed the towel back on the shelf. Then she stood, but stayed bent at the waist, examining the ground around her. "There's more over here. It doesn't look like a lot, but enough to have me worried."

"Uncle Nick? What's going on?"

Nick whirled. "Lindsey! Where did you come from?"

"The bathroom." She pointed in the direction of the safe area. Through the door, Nick could see the other door that led to the restroom. Lindsey's fingers twisted together. "I was in there. What's wrong?"

Nick shot a look at Carly and grabbed the girl's hand.

"They must have grabbed him while she was in the bathroom."

She gave an agonized nod. "They picked the kid who would give them the least trouble."

Heart in his throat, he said, "Come on, we need to get someone tracking that car as soon as possible." To Lindsey, he said, "They've got Christopher, honey, but we're going to get him back safe and sound, okay?"

The girl's eyes went wide. Then she started crying.

As he turned to usher her back to the house, a low moan reached his ears.

Carly must have heard it, too, as she froze and shot him a look.

Reaching for her weapon, she held it ready as she approached the utility storage cabinet that leaned against the wall on the other side of the garage.

Another groan and a grunt came from it.

Nick pushed Lindsey toward the door and silently motioned for her to run back to the house. "Go," he whispered.

She took two steps then looked back, fear for him clearly displayed on her sweet face. Not wanting to let her out of his sight, he hesitated, then pointed and mouthed, "Now."

She'd be safer with the authorities in the house. He wasn't worried about any bad guys still hanging around. They'd gotten what they'd come for and were long gone by now.

Lindsey pivoted on one foot and raced to safety. Nick followed Carly. If someone came out of that thing with a weapon, she wasn't going to face it alone.

Shoulders tense, he watched her step to the side of the cabinet door. She motioned him to the other side. He did as she silently instructed, their actions taking him back to his police training.

He pointed to the side of the cabinet. Stained a dark red. More blood.

Carly reached for the handle, twisted it and flung the door open.

A man stumbled out and fell to the floor at her feet.

Nick breathed a little easier as he realized it was the officer who'd been sent to watch over the children and Debbie.

A gash on his forehead had started to clot, and his nose looked like it had been broken. Multiple bruises covered the left side of his face.

Carly holstered her gun and knelt beside the young man. Looking up at Nick, she tossed him her phone. "Call for help, will you?"

Nick dialed 9-1-1. He had to stop and ask for the address, and Carly supplied it while she checked the officer's pulse. "Strong and steady. Ben, you're going to be all right." She patted the unblemished side of his face, trying to get him to open his eyes. They fluttered, and she asked, "Can you tell me what happened?"

"Help's on the way," Nick interrupted. "I imagine Lindsey's inside telling everyone what's going on, too."

"Good." She looked back at the officer. "Come on, Ben, wake up a little and tell me what happened."

With a groan, Ben licked his lips then said, "They... um...jumped me. They picked the lock on the door or something...I don't know. They hit me with something... pushed me." Another groan. "My head." His eyes fluttered shut, then opened again. "They hit Debbie, too, and grabbed the kid. I...tried to stop...them...I did..." He faded again, and this time Carly let him go.

Nick watched her in action. She was very good at her job. Efficient, courageous, lovely. And in a profession that could get her killed.

He shuddered at the thought.

And Christopher. Anguish twisted through him. And Debbie, too. Two people he'd promised to keep safe. What was he going to tell Wayne? Guilt flooded him, and he had to shove away the awful images that came to his mind.

Debbie and Christopher were fine until he had evidence stating otherwise.

Noise from the door leading from the house captured his attention. A team entered the garage, and Carly said, "Ben's hurt. I've got an ambulance on the way. They've got Christopher and Debbie. There's blood in the garage. I want to know who it belongs to."

A rapid explanation brought everyone up to date on what had just happened right under their noses. Nick's terror knew no limits.

Making his way back into the house, he and Carly left the officer to the attention of the paramedics who'd just arrived. Lindsey threw herself into his arms, and he hugged her tight. Then she twisted, launched herself onto the couch and sobbed. Carly made her way to her and clutched the girl's hand, whispering soothing words. Nick was so lost in his fear, he couldn't understand a word she said.

Instead of trying to listen, he walked into the bedroom he was supposed to share with Christopher that night and fell to his knees beside the bed.

Head in his hands, he cried out to the One who knew exactly where Chris was. "Oh, God, protect him. He's just a little boy." Grief and fear stole his breath, and he couldn't form any more words. What had the blood in the garage meant? Did it belong to Christopher or Debbie? Who had walked right in and stolen part of his family?

"Please, Lord, please," was all he could choke out of a throat tightened by sheer terror for the child he loved.

Behind him, he heard Lindsey's sobs fade while Carly

barked orders. "Find out how to track the car that was in the garage. We've got to find them fast."

Nick knew what she was thinking. He was thinking the same thing.

What the crushed inhaler in the satin-lined box meant for a terrified seven-year-old boy.

Carly sipped her coffee and studied the flickering television set from her seat at the kitchen table. They'd come full circle. Back in Nicholas's house, they waited.

For something.

A note. A phone call. An e-mail. Anything.

She pictured the scene at the safe house and replayed the last few minutes after Christopher had been snatched right out from under them.

Light, almost soundless footsteps, crossed the floor behind her. When she turned, she spotted Lindsey eyeing her. "Hi."

"Hi." The girl's eyes dropped to the floor.

"Nice outfit. Love the wig," Carly teased.

That brought a slight smile as she fingered a dark tress that hung over her right shoulder. "I was going to be in a play the day we had to leave school early. I was a Roman emperor's wife."

"I'm sure you would have done a fabulous job."

"Yes, I would have," the girl agreed without a hint of bragging. She was just stating a fact. "I stuffed it in my backpack as we were being shoved into the car. I just felt like putting it on for some reason."

Probably wishing she was someone else, Carly mused to herself. Someone not even remotely connected to the case or anyone who had anything to do with it. She felt sympathy tug her heart and asked, "Is there something you wanted to talk to me about?"

A nod.

Carly stood and walked over to the couch and patted the seat beside her. "Come here."

Lindsey walked around the couch and settled beside Carly, her eyes still lowered.

Carly could almost hear her mind clicking. She took Lindsey's cool hand in her own. "You're freezing." Grabbing the blanket off the cushion behind her, she wrapped it around the girl's shoulders and waited, giving her time.

Did she remember something else from yesterday?

Lindsey sighed. "I don't understand God sometimes."

Oh, no, not a God conversation. "I know, honey, I don't, either."

"But I still believe in Him, you know?"

"Your uncle does, too."

"Do you?" This time Lindsey's eyes lifted and stared deep into Carly's as though trying to read her very soul.

There wasn't going to be any lying to this girl. Carly took a deep breath. "I don't know, Lindsey. I'm having a tough time with God right now." She looked away and stared out the window. "I see a lot of bad stuff in my job, Lindsey. And six months ago I had a very close friend who was killed."

"I'm sorry," Lindsey whispered.

"Yeah," Carly nodded and looked back at her. "I am, too. He meant a lot to me. I grew up with a great dad and a pretty cool big brother, and Hank was as close to me as they are. It was like losing a family member." She blew out a sigh and wondered if she was sharing too much with the young girl. And yet, she didn't want to treat her like a kid when Lindsey was acting like a mature adult. "I guess it's because his death was so unnecessary and…" She gave a shrug. "I suppose I feel like God could have prevented it, you know?"

"But He didn't." A flat statement.

"No. He didn't." Carly felt the familiar lump form in her throat and swallowed.

"I know how you feel."

Carly squeezed the fragile fingers. "Your mom and aunt?"

"Yes," Lindsey whispered. "I thought God must have hated me to take them away from me like that."

"Oh, sweetie, God doesn't hate you. He loves you very much."

A sad, too-mature smile crossed Lindsey's lips. "I know. At least I used to. I'm not so sure anymore. Not with Christopher gone now." Two big tears spilled over and down her cheeks. "Things were just starting to get better, and now this."

Carly pulled the girl into a hug, and Lindsey sighed then gave a hiccup. "But if all the bad stuff hadn't happened, we wouldn't have met you. And I'm glad you're here. So I think maybe even when the bad stuff happens, God lets good stuff happen, too, so we don't totally lose our faith, you know?"

Carly went still. "Good stuff in the midst of the bad?"

"Yeah, something like that, I guess." She shrugged then stood. "I don't know. I'm going back to my room. I want to be alone for a while."

"Okay, hon." Carly let her go, her mind reeling with what Lindsey had just said. She thought back. Had anything good happened in the midst of all the bad?

When Hank had been killed, what good had come from that?

His widow had been left with a hefty sum of life insurance, and the house that had been in the process of foreclosure was paid off. Not the way she'd wanted to do it, but if Hank had to die...

Carly rubbed her eyes.

"You okay?"

She looked up. Mason stood with the laptop in his hand. She waved him over. "What's up?"

"Come here. I want to show you something." Carly walked into the kitchen and took the chair she'd vacated when Lindsey had claimed her attention.

Mason sat in the chair next to her and placed the computer on the table. "Our officer's name is Ben McCann."

Footsteps sounded, and she turned. Nicholas descended the stairs looking like he'd aged ten years in the last six hours since Christopher's disappearance.

Without a word, he sat beside her and poured himself a cup of coffee. She wanted to ask him how he was but figured that would be a dumb question. She wanted to hug him, hold him, tell him everything would be all right.

But she just didn't know. Looking away from him, her heart aching like someone had reached in and punched it, she fixed her gaze on Mason and asked, "Yeah, and? Does Ben McCann have a story?" She felt numb inside but knew it wouldn't last. Soon fear, guilt, shame, and more would invade her to the depths of her very being. But for now, she would take the numbness. It wouldn't distract her like the other feelings would.

"A good cop of four years. Nothing negative on his record. But he's in debt up to his ears."

"Do you think they bought him off? Knocked him out to make us think he didn't have anything to do with it?"

"Looks like it. He just deposited ten grand into his checking account yesterday."

"Something to definitely check into. When he wakes up from that nasty concussion I'm sure he's got, I want to hear what he has to say for himself. What made you do a background check on him?"

A shrug. "I'm checking everyone."

She rubbed her eyes. "Okay, but how did they even get to the garage? It's wide open out there. We had people watching the grounds. How would they get from the edge of the woods to that garage without someone seeing them?"

"A good question. Unfortunately, I don't have a good answer." Mason tapped a few more keys, then said, "If they watched the movements for a while, they may have picked up on a pattern, waited for a break then made their move."

"And everything happened so quietly. Lindsey didn't hear a thing from the bathroom."

"If the door was shut, she probably wouldn't."

In a sudden movement, Nick set his cup on the table and wondered aloud, "Why haven't they called?"

At first Carly didn't speak. Then she drew in a deep breath and looked at him. "Because they don't have to. You know what they want."

He nodded. "Yeah. I do."

"How's Lindsey?"

"Asleep. Finally."

"She's feeling guilty, isn't she?"

He lifted a brow in surprise. "Yes, she is. I tried telling her it wasn't her fault, but I don't think she hears me."

"She will. Just don't give up telling her." A pause. "I'm sorry, Nick."

"It's not your fault, Carly."

"I failed you. I failed myself. I..." Now the emotion swarmed her, and she did her best to beat it back. Through her tears, she saw Nick shoot a look at Mason.

Mason nodded and rose to disappear outside, where he would walk the perimeter.

Nick scooted his chair over and put his arm around her

shoulder. "You didn't fail, Carly. It's not your fault any more than it's Lindsey's."

Jerking away from him, she stood and stumbled over to the sink. She felt a tear slide down her cheek. Furious at her unprofessional behavior, she turned her back on him and swiped at the wetness.

But he wouldn't let her withdraw from him. Pulling her around to face him, he stared deep into her eyes, into her soul. "You're blaming God, aren't you?"

She looked away, desperately trying to keep the tears from falling.

"Aren't you?" he insisted.

"Yes!" she hissed. "Yes, I am. He's a seven-year-old little boy, Nick. It's not right! Where is the justice in this world anymore? Where? Where's God when stuff like this happens? Why does He let good men with so much to live for get killed? Why wouldn't He intervene when someone enters a house with the intention of kidnapping a little boy in order to force his uncle to—" She broke off because her voice wouldn't work anymore. Sobs crowded her throat, clamoring to get out. But she wouldn't let them. She wouldn't.

For a moment Nick didn't answer. Then she felt his arms slide around her and pull her to him.

The sobs won. She let them out and poured them onto his strong chest.

She felt him plant a light kiss on her hair and felt ashamed at the comfort it gave her. She pulled away and ordered herself to get it together. "I'm sorry, Nick. I'm so sorry. I'll find someone else to take over for me. I'm not able to handle this. I'm being completely unprofessional, and you need someone—" Her voice squeaked and broke again.

Hands cupped her face, and she looked into his eyes. "I

need you, Carly. And you need to do this. To see it through to the end. Just like I have to do."

"But—"

"Shh…." He placed a finger over her lips. "No buts. God is in control. I can't see His plan. I don't understand why He lets this kind of thing happen, but I trust Him. Do you get that? I really do trust Him. I have to."

"But Chris…"

He closed his eyes, and when he opened them, tears swam there. "I won't say I'm not scared for him. I'm not saying I'm going to like the way this ends, but…" He drew in a deep breath, "I will trust Him. In all things. In all His ways. Okay?"

She shook her head. "I can't do that."

His forehead touched hers. "Yes, you can, Carly. It's not just a heart decision. It's a head decision. One you have to make over and over, again and again. And it's not easy. But it is real. God is real, His promises are true, and He'll get us through this no matter what."

"I want to believe that. I really do." Surprisingly enough, she found she did. She thought back to the brief prayer she'd uttered earlier and the comfort it had given her.

"Then believe it. Ask Him to help you believe it."

Biting her lip, she pulled away from him and walked back to the kitchen table to pick up her coffee. She took a sip and grimaced at the lukewarm liquid. Without looking at him, she said, "I'll try."

A hand reached out and grasped her chin. She looked up. "That's all He asks. For your willingness to be open to Him."

She nodded. "Okay. If you can trust Him in this situation, I can at least be willing to listen if He has something to say to me."

Nick pulled her to him for a hug, and Carly felt her heart break as she tried to communicate the prayer in her soul. *Please, God, bring Christopher home safe and sound. Help me to believe.*

TWELVE

It had been twenty-six hours since Christopher and Debbie's disappearance, and Nick felt each minute age him. They'd decided against going public with the kidnappings.

Even the FBI had agreed in this instance. They knew who had Chris and Debbie; they just didn't know where, and it was a sure bet they wouldn't be making any public appearances.

So the less the media knew, the better.

When he'd called Wayne Thomas with the news, the man had gone silent then said, "I'm coming over. If we're all in one place, it'll be easier to keep abreast of everything."

Nick had agreed.

Wayne had arrived and planted himself on the couch, his eagle eye taking in every detail of the FBI operation now in charge of locating Christopher and Debbie. They'd invaded Nick's house shortly after he'd arrived home yesterday. Nick and Carly had discussed asking the man about Debbie's association with a de Lugo thug. She promised to get to that at the right moment. He wondered what she was waiting for.

Carly walked into the den and headed toward him. Wayne looked up from the laptop he'd brought. Carly rubbed her hands together and looked at them. "I just got word that the blood on the floor of the garage at the safe house is Debbie's."

Blood drained from Wayne's face, but he just nodded. Nick reached out and gripped his friend's arm. "I'm sorry, Wayne."

Wayne looked at him, sorrow in his eyes. "It's not your fault, and it wasn't that much blood. Right? Maybe they just hit her to keep her quiet and..." He shrugged and looked away.

Nick looked at Carly, who bit her lip. She'd had trouble looking him in the eye after her meltdown, but he'd refused to let her ignore him. And he thought he saw a new peace in her eyes. At least he hoped so. Once all this was over, he looked forward to discussing it further.

Carly cleared her throat and frowned. Nick raised a brow. "What is it?"

"The blood on the cabinet belongs to Ben."

"You kind of figured that, didn't you?"

"Yes, that one doesn't surprise me." She paused. "But we still don't know how they keep staying one step ahead of us. It seems to me we're missing something."

"Like what?"

She placed her hands on her hips and cocked her head. "That's the problem. I can't figure it out." Looking at Nick, she asked, "How would Ben McCann have access to secure information like the location of the different safe houses kept by the marshals?"

"He wouldn't. There's no way."

"Yeah, that's what I would think, but someone did, and someone must have done their homework on the most likely cop to buy off."

"The most likely cop that had access to us," Nick said slowly. Wayne watched the action, his eyes bouncing back and forth.

Carly paced over to Mason and asked, "Any more on the background checks?"

He looked at her. "Maria and Grady came up clean, of course."

Guilt appeared on her face, and Nick wanted to tell her not to worry about it. She was just doing her job, and he appreciated that fact even while he didn't like the danger involved with it.

"I figured they would," she said. "I was desperate and grasping at straws."

"How are they doing, by the way?" Nick asked.

Mason gave him a thumbs-up. "On the road to recovery. Maria's already home. Grady's made amazing strides, and is supposed to be released in the next couple of days."

Carly fidgeted then rolled her eyes. "Um, can we keep this whole background-check thing between us?"

A slight smile curved her partner's lips. "That's what I'd planned on."

"Okay…so, Ben McCann. Someone had to have access to his records. Bank records, personal stuff, et cetera."

"That kind of stuff takes a court order," Nick offered. "They'd have had to get that just like we did."

She nodded her approval. "True. Unless you get it illegally."

Nick shuddered. "They knew exactly when we got here, when to plant the package…"

Carly picked up when he trailed off. "They also had to know the layout of the house and know we'd probably send all of you to the safe area, so that's where they planned their strike."

"Only," Nick said slowly, the wheels turning, "how did they know I would refuse to go back there? How did they know to send the inhaler, and how did they know they'd be able to grab Christopher?"

"Coincidence," Mason interjected. "They probably sent the inhaler as a message. It just so happened that you didn't go to the safe area, so they grabbed Christopher and Debbie instead of killing you."

He blew out a sigh. "Why take Debbie?"

"To keep Christopher quiet," Carly murmured. "If he's with someone he trusts, he's less likely to cause problems."

"Or the de Lugos somehow convinced her to help them out."

Carly stared out the window and listened to the men behind her discuss the situation. Her eyes roamed the area, alert for anything out of place. Yet she was also focused on her thoughts. Christopher had been snatched right from under their noses.

She paced to the sofa and sat, then leaned her head back against the cushion to glare at the ceiling. How was this possible? How could this be happening? Should she ask for a replacement like she suggested to Nick and remove herself from the case? He said she needed to see this thing through to the end. Carly wasn't so sure. The end of this case might just bring the end to her sanity.

All of these questions buzzed in her mind, but the one that screamed the loudest was: *Is this your fault?*

Was it?

Could she have prevented this?

Of course you could have, she sneered at herself. *You're a professional, remember? You're supposed to be smarter than the bad guys.*

But, she silently argued back, *how can I fight the bad guys when I can't tell them apart from the good ones?*

Carly felt the tears clog her throat and forced them away.

God, what do You want from me? her mind cried out in desperation. *What do You want?*

She thought about Nick and his fervent prayers to the God he believed in, the God he trusted. He made it look so easy.

Could she do that? Be like Nick and just trust that God knew best even in this dire situation?

She wanted to with all of her aching, shattered heart. "Please," she whispered silently. "Show me."

"Hey, Carly? You in there?" Mason snapped his fingers in front of her eyes, and she bolted from the couch, fists clenched. With a deep breath, she forced herself to relax.

"Sorry, deep thoughts."

Nick frowned and shot her a concerned look. "Are you all right?"

She didn't bother to answer that. Instead she looked at Mason. "What were you saying?"

"I said we just got word back on the condition of Ben McCann."

Eagerness filled her. Finally they would learn more. "Well? Is he awake? Can he tell us anything?"

"Afraid not. He died thirty minutes ago. Started bleeding in his brain, had a stroke and died."

Carly felt the breath *whoosh* from her and fell back onto the couch. A groan slipped out, and she placed her face in her hands. But her mind clicked. She didn't have time to fall apart.

Shoving her emotions aside, she took a restoring breath and said, "Okay. Then we just have to keep looking, keep searching until we find the answer to Christopher and Debbie's whereabouts."

Something tickled the back of her mind. She just couldn't pull it forward enough to grab it.

It would come to her.

She looked at Mason. "We need the reports back on the safe houses."

"It's too soon, Carly. They probably haven't even finished processing them."

He was right. She was going to have to be a little more patient. Still...

"This will be a priority case right now. They'll be moving fast on the evidence they have. Not to mention the fact that the people missing belong to two judges."

"That's true. Give it a try. Sure can't hurt."

She picked up her phone, walked into the kitchen and dialed the captain's number. From where she stood, she could see Nick and Wayne sitting on the couch talking. Probably about the de Lugo trial that started tomorrow.

"Captain Sanders."

"Hi, Captain. Carly Masterson here. I know it's been a short time, but is there anything you or one of your people can tell me about the safe houses we left? Was the gas leak an accident or on purpose?"

"You're in luck. Because the trial is fast approaching and I know you need all the information you can get as fast as you can get it, I had two teams working each of the houses. I just got off the phone with my lead investigator about the gas leak. It looks like a simple accident that could have been deadly if you hadn't recognized the smell."

That surprised her. "How so?"

"The leak came from the stove. The gas line that leads to the back of the stove had come loose. It had probably worked its way loose over time, and whenever someone was messing with the stove yesterday morning, it pulled enough so the bolt fell off and a large amount of gas was released. Once it hit the air-conditioning duct, it would have traveled fairly quickly to all areas of the house."

Which explained why Lindsey had come from the bedroom feeling sick.

"How did you know it was a gas leak?" he asked.

"I don't know, sir. It just popped into my head. I don't have a gas stove at home, but that smell, combined with the way I was feeling physically..." She gave a shrug he couldn't see.

"Well, good call. You're lucky."

Very. "Okay, thanks so much."

"One other thing."

"What's that?"

"We found a cell phone tucked up under the lawn mower in the garage."

"A cell phone? How odd. Who does it belong to?"

"Debbie Thomas."

Carly frowned. "What? Debbie Thomas? But that's not possible. I took her phone from her at the first safe house."

"Well, that brings me to this bit of information. There wasn't a phone in the drawer at that safe house. Which leads me to deduce that the cell phone you had in the drawer is now in our possession."

Chills of foreboding danced across her skin, and goose bumps made an abrupt appearance. "How can that be? I took it from her, pulled the battery out and put it in the drawer."

"We didn't find the inhaler, either."

Confused, Carly thought for a moment, then said, "All right. Thanks, Captain. I'm going to try to figure out what all this means. I'll be in touch."

"Good deal. Stay safe."

"Right." Carly hung up, her mind spinning with this latest bit of news.

She still felt like she was missing something.

"Carly?"

At the sound of Nick's voice, she snapped to her attention and found him standing on the opposite side of the bar. She leaned against the granite countertop and studied him as he settled onto a bar stool. She said, "I'm not sure what it all means yet, but they didn't find the phone or the inhaler."

Nick frowned and leaned forward. "But I know I had the spare one in there. I grabbed the one in the kitchen on the way out and..." He scratched his head, thinking. "Yes, I'm absolutely sure the other one was in the medicine cabinet. I put it there in case Christopher had an attack and I needed it fast. I didn't want to have to go digging around in a bag to find it."

"And I know where I put the phone."

"So, did Debbie somehow snatch it before we left?"

Carly sighed and noticed Wayne, Debbie's father, following the conversation. When he saw he had their attention, he rose and joined them in the kitchen. "They found Debbie's phone?"

Carly nodded, and a sick look flashed across the man's face as he looked away for a moment. Then he turned back. "All right. So, what does this mean?"

"We're not sure yet," Carly said. "But I want to ask you a question." She figured this was the moment. She hadn't wanted to bring it up before in case it was irrelevant. Now she had to ask.

"About?" Wayne prompted.

"Debbie. What do you know about her association with Rico Martinez?"

Annoyance flashed for a brief moment. Then he shrugged. "She dated him. He's good-looking, wealthy and to all appearances is from one of the most influential families in the area. She didn't care about his associations until he nearly landed her in jail. It took some doing to get her out of that one, I'll admit." He narrowed his eyes. "How did you find out about that? I thought I covered it up pretty well."

Mason spoke up. "You did. I had to do some heavy-duty digging to find it."

"Why are you checking up on my daughter? Nick? Something you need to tell me?" His brow shot up, and Nick looked flustered.

Carly rushed to his assistance. "Because we couldn't seem to find a hiding place without being discovered almost immediately, we did background checks on everyone associated with this family."

Wayne shook his head. "Well, I can't say I blame you. But that's the story on Debbie and Martinez. She didn't know what she was getting into when she started seeing him. I knew the behind-the-scene story, of course, and shared it with her." He gave a humorless laugh. "At first she wouldn't listen to a word I had to say about a de Lugo associate, but once he was arrested for extortion and they tried to make her an accomplice, she realized I was right and dropped him like a hot potato."

He blew out a sigh. "Look, I'm going crazy just sitting around here waiting. I have some things at the office I need to take care of. Nick has my number. Please call me as soon as you hear anything."

"Of course."

She and Nick watched Wayne gather his belongings and head out the door.

When the man was gone, Carly paced. Nick said, "Excuse me, I'm going to check on Lindsey," and slipped away.

At her wits' end, Carly grabbed a notepad and a pen and settled herself at the kitchen table. Sometimes it helped if she made lists or scribbled down the facts she knew in order to visualize everything.

Starting with Nick, she wrote down everything she could think of about the man.

- Good uncle/family man who loves his niece and nephew.
- A judge unwavering in his integrity and principles.
- Well respected in his peer circle.
- A man to admire.
- Handles himself well under pressure.
- Strong in his faith.

Not sure where she was going with this, she stopped. That last one stared back at her. With her pen, she circled the word *faith*.

Where had her faith gone?

She hadn't ditched it all at once. Her disbelief that God took a personal interest in what she was going through had snuck up on her.

So, what did she really believe?

Did He care or not?

Lindsey said she believed even after all she'd been through in her twelve short years. Nick said he did even though his nephew had been snatched out from under the noses of law enforcement. Not only that, but Nick hadn't hurled one insult, one word of blame—at her or God.

Why not?

She sure would have. But Nick talked about God like He was a best friend. She asked herself the same question she'd asked earlier.

Could she do the same?

Taking a deep breath, she decided to give it a shot. *God? I can't believe I'm saying this, but I've missed You. I want to believe You care, I really do, but it's so hard to see it sometimes. Especially right now, with Christopher and Debbie missing. Could You just...um...do something? Keep them safe? Show us who keeps leading the bad guys to us.*

She sat still and waited. Nothing.

This time.

But she still remembered the prayer she'd uttered at the safe house. And the peace she'd felt—even in the midst of her grief and anger—after unloading on Nick once they'd arrived back at his house.

Maybe she should keep trying and see what happened.

Okay, God, if that's what I need to do to find You, I'll do it.

Picking up the pen once more, she wrote:

Debbie Thomas:
- Nanny.
- Cares about Nick and the kids.
- Probably thinks she's in love with Nick.
- Cell phone?
- Went back to get it?
- What about the inhaler?
- Taken with Christopher from safe house number two.
- Dated a man with a known connection to the de Lugo family. Coincidence or not?
- But she quit seeing him after she found out about his mob connections, right? Or did she?

* * *

The facts and questions stared back at her. What was she thinking? That the answers would just leap off the page? She wished.

Back to the inhaler that had been in the bathroom medicine cabinet.

Was Nick right? Or had he grabbed it during their frantic departure and just not remembered?

Possibly.

Or had Debbie forgotten the one on the kitchen counter because she'd already gotten the one from the bathroom?

But *why* would she do that?

"What are you doing?" Mason's question startled her.

"Thinking."

"About what?"

"This case. What else?"

"I thought you might be thinking about a particular judge."

Carly eyed him and then figured why hide it. "He is the case, remember?" But she knew what he meant. And he knew she knew. "I can't have any romantic feelings for him until this job is finished."

Mason grinned. "Oh, you can have the feelings." His smile slid off. "But I admire you for not acting on them."

A sigh blew through her pursed lips. "How come you and I never got together?"

Mason patted her on the head. "Because there aren't any romantic feelings."

"Thanks a lot, Stone," Carly grunted.

"You're welcome, Masterson." He headed toward the door. "I'm going to walk the grounds."

"Are the dogs back?"

"No, the Jeffersons took them with them."

"Be careful. They only have one more chance to get Nick, and that's tonight."

Mason opened the door and lifted one side of his mouth. "The thought had occurred to me."

"Right."

After Mason left, Carly pondered the sheet of paper in front of her again. Slowly, an idea formed, but it was so outrageous she wondered if she should just ignore it.

If she was wrong, she could be in a lot of trouble.

But if she was right...

Standing, she headed for the stairs. She needed to talk to Nicholas.

THIRTEEN

At the top of the stairs, Carly made a left and walked down the carpeted hall to Nicholas's study. Whispers reached her ears and she slowed, placed her hand on her gun and approached the cracked door.

Who would be whispering?

Nick?

Lindsey?

She gave the door a gentle shove, and it opened without a sound.

The whispering continued.

Peeking around the doorjamb, she saw Nicholas at his desk, head in his hands, Bible open in front of him.

But he wasn't reading. He was whispering. Prayers.

Heart thumping, Carly removed her hand from her gun. Not wanting to intrude on his privacy, she stepped back.

The floor creaked, and Nick's head shot up. Tears glistened in his eyes, and he quickly blinked them away.

Carly raised a hand. "I'm sorry, Nick, I came to talk to you, and when I saw you—" she motioned toward the Bible "—I was trying to back off without disturbing you."

Nick shook his head. "It's all right, Carly. Come on in."

Still hesitating, she waited until he waved her in a

second time. Making her way into the study, she took a good look around her. She'd been in this room when she'd done sweeps of the house, but now she paid more attention to the details.

Pictures of the kids. A picture of his parents. One of Miriam. Carly picked it up. "She was beautiful."

"Yes, she was. Inside and out—when we first met."

"You said she changed."

A deep sigh echoed through the room as he nodded and said, "After we were married, my career really took off. I spent less and less time at home, and she spent more and more time alone."

"That's tough."

"It was. And then she decided she wanted a baby." He shrugged. "That was fine with me. I've always wanted children, and when Miriam approached me with the idea, I got excited at the thought."

"And then she couldn't get pregnant."

Nick shook his head. "No. She couldn't."

"And that's when she started to change?"

"Yeah." He tapped his lips thoughtfully. "Yeah."

"And then she died in the car accident."

At the word *accident,* Nick's jaw tightened, and he scoffed. "Accident. I don't think so, but I can't prove it. And before you ask, yes, I've tried. Called in special favors and everything. Although, from what's been said in the threats this time, I know I'm right." He went quiet for a few moments, and Carly replaced the picture on the shelf.

Clearing her throat, she asked, "What are you doing?"

"Praying."

"It helps, doesn't it?" She didn't know why she asked. It was obvious it did. But she wanted to hear it again, hear him explain why he relied on God when it looked like God had totally pushed Nick to the spiritual back burner.

Because when Nick said it helped, it gave her hope. Like maybe God was listening to her, too.

He frowned down at the Bible, but she knew he didn't see it, wasn't frowning at the book. "Yes. It helps. Although, to be honest, right now it's hard to be still and listen to whatever God wants to say to me."

"Why's that?"

The heels of his palms scrubbed his eyes. When he focused back on her, he gave a sad little grimace and said, "Because I'm too busy begging Him to spare Christopher's life."

Her throat clogged. "I can understand that."

"Will you pray with me?"

Strangely enough, she wasn't repelled by the idea. Instead, she was honored that he'd asked. "Sure, Nick, I'll pray with you."

He took her hand, and she bowed her head. Her heart thumped in her chest as he talked to God in a way that revealed he did this often. When he whispered "Amen," Carly repeated the prayer's closing and looked into Nick's eyes. "I want to believe."

"Then just do it."

She took a deep breath. "Okay."

He blinked. "What?"

"Okay. I'm choosing to believe God's going to work this out. I'm choosing to put my faith in Him once more."

"And if things don't work out like we want them to? What will you believe then?"

Tears filled her eyes. "Then I'll just have to believe that God knows best. I want to keep the faith even in the hard times, even in the times when I don't understand why things happen the way they do. I want to believe He's still in control anyway."

Nick leaned his forehead against hers and breathed, "He is." Then he finally, gently placed his lips against hers, and Carly reveled in the feeling. She slid her arms around his neck and kissed him back.

Then reality hit. She jerked away and stared up at him wide-eyed. "I can't kiss you."

"I'm sorry." He closed his eyes and ran a hand over his hair. "You must think I'm awful…with Christopher still missing and—"

"No, no, no. I don't think that at all. I think you're hurting, scared, unsure of the future and looking for comfort. And I think that's okay. But right now, we need our heads clear and focused."

Relief glistened in his eyes. "Thanks for that." Nick squeezed her hand, and Carly marveled at the sweet sensations stirring within her.

Pulling her hand from his, she cleared her throat, focused her thoughts and said, "I've got an idea, and I want to run it by you."

"Okay."

"Do you still have Christopher's things that were brought back here from the safe house?"

He flinched at the mention of Christopher, but it couldn't be helped. He nodded. "They're still in his little suitcase in his room. On his bed."

"Come on. Let's take a look at them."

Confused, but willing to go with whatever Carly thought she knew, Nick followed her down the hall to Chris's bedroom. Just entering the room sent chills down his spine and terror racing through his heart.

What would he do if God chose to let Christopher die?

What would he do if he never again saw the little boy's impish grin and dancing gray eyes he'd inherited from his mother?

The thought made him light-headed for a moment. Then he realized Carly was speaking to him.

"Nick, are you all right?"

"No. No, I'm not." Deep breath. "But I will be. What do you need?"

She unzipped the little suitcase decorated with dancing monkeys. "I want you to look in here and tell me if anything is missing."

His brows slammed together. "Missing?"

"Yes."

Wanting to drill her about why she needed that information, but knowing he probably needed to answer her first, he pulled the clothes out of the bag and set them on the bed. They'd been packed in a hurry, just shoved in the suitcase. He sorted through them, piece by piece.

It didn't take long.

His hand paused above the empty suitcase. "His yellow muscle shirt and black shorts are missing. Along with a pair of underwear. He was wearing his flip-flops when he was in the safe area." He looked up at her. "How did you know?" The sick look on her face caused his heart to thump. "Carly?"

"I don't know anything yet. It's just a suspicion, and I might be completely wrong. I need to find out if the clothing was just overlooked or deliberately taken."

"Taken? By whom? The person who kidnapped him? But who would have time—or access?"

She looked at him. "That's what I'm going to find out. Are you absolutely sure that you left Christopher's inhaler in the bathroom medicine cabinet?"

"Yes." He closed his eyes and did his best to remember

his actions. "We got there, and I pulled it out of the bag because if Christopher had an attack I wanted to be able to go straight to it and grab it." He opened his eyes and looked into hers. "I promise, Carly, that's where I left it."

"Okay. Then it's time for me to do a little more digging."

"Tell me who you suspect." Jaw clenched, he stood firm. This was his nephew. He had a right to know.

"No." She pulled her hand from his and propped both hands on her hips to meet him stare for stare. "I could be wrong. Until I find out for sure..." She held up a hand even as she cut off her own words.

"Carly..."

"I mean it, Nick. I'll tell you as soon as I find out if I'm right."

A muscle jumped in his jaw, and he tried to relax his gritted teeth. He managed just enough to mutter, "Fine."

"Thanks. Now—" she paced to the door "—I need to see Lindsey's bag."

He didn't bother asking why, she noticed, just walked out the door and down the hall. She followed. Lindsey sat on her bed reading a book. She lifted a brow as they entered. "What is it?"

"I need to see your suitcase. Have you unpacked it?"

"Yes, why?"

"Was there anything missing from it?"

Her lips formed a disgusted frown. "Yes, one of my wigs. I must have left it somewhere." Then she shrugged. "Guess it doesn't really matter. The play is long over now. I don't need them now."

Carly smiled in sympathy. "Anything else?"

"A pink T-shirt. That's all. I don't care. I didn't really like that shirt anyway."

"Thanks."

They left the room, and before Nick could jump on her with the questions raging in him, she asked him, "What are you going to do about tomorrow?"

The very question he'd been agonizing over, begging God for clear direction.

He stared her in the eye. "I don't know. I may not know until I walk into the courthouse tomorrow."

She met his gaze without blinking. "All right. Then I'll let you get back to your study. I've got some questions I've got to hunt down answers for."

He nodded. "I'm going to check on Lindsey one more time then try to rest."

He needed rest. He couldn't remember the last time he'd gotten more than two consecutive hours of good sleep. Not that he expected to do much better tonight.

Not with Christopher and Debbie still missing.

He watched Carly head back down the stairs and went back to say good night to Lindsey.

He found her curled on her bed, staring at the wall. She wasn't reading anymore. Instead, she looked heartbroken.

Grief stole his breath and nearly brought him to his knees. Lindsey had never been an exuberant child even before her mother's death. After his sister died, Lindsey had withdrawn into herself, protecting herself by keeping her distance from those she loved as though afraid she might be hurt by losing someone else.

Over the past year, she'd made progress with the help of a good counselor, learning to deal with her mother's death, learning to trust Nick, drawing closer to him even with the adolescent attitude.

And she loved and protected Christopher in a way that showed she was intimately familiar with losing a loved one.

Now her little brother had disappeared. It didn't take a psychologist to know how she was feeling.

"Hey, Linds."

"Hey." She didn't move, but at least she responded.

"It's not your fault."

"I should have protected him, Uncle Nick. I shouldn't have left him alone."

Her anguish broke his heart. Sitting beside her, he took her hand in his and kissed the knuckles. "That wasn't your responsibility, Linds, even though you took on that role. I've never seen a sister who loved her brother more."

A sob suddenly shook her, and she sat up to wind her arms around his neck. "I'm sorry, Uncle Nick, I'm sorry." Her tears soaked his shoulder in record time.

"Lindsey, you don't have anything to apologize for."

"But I didn't see what happened. I didn't even hear anything."

"You were in another part of the building, darling. That's no surprise."

"He's got to be so scared, and I can't do anything about it." More sobs shook her thin frame. A frame that he now noticed had lost a few pounds she couldn't afford to lose.

A lump formed in his throat, and it was a minute before he could speak. "I know, hon, I know." A pause. "But I don't think he's that scared." God forgive him for lying. "Debbie's with him, remember? She's probably holding him. Comforting him. I think he's probably okay."

"But you don't know that, do you?"

"No, but it's what I'm praying for. She loves Christopher, and I think the people that took Chris took Debbie to help with him. You see?"

At first she didn't say anything. Then she gave a slow nod. "Yes. I see. I hope that's true."

"Wanna pray about it?"

"Yeah. I do."

* * *

Carly watched the sun come up, her thoughts on little Christopher, Debbie and, of course, Nicholas. The night had passed without incident. What would Nick do today? Sit on the bench or recuse himself? She honestly didn't know what he planned to do. She didn't think he knew, either.

The phone rang in the distance, and Carly heard the FBI agents scrambling to make sure they got a tape of whoever was calling. Nerves taught, she stood next to one of the agents, whose name she couldn't remember. "Who is it?"

The woman pulled off the earpiece. "Wayne Thomas." Nick took it.

Carly made her way to the kitchen and looked down at the list she'd made the night before. The idea she'd had last night came back in full force.

"Mason," she called.

He came in from the den. "Yeah?"

"Keep an eye on Nick. I have an idea I want to check out."

"Want to share it?"

Did she? What if she was wrong?

What if she was right?

Still, she hesitated. "Just keep your phone on. I may be completely off base, but I need to make sure, okay?"

"Where are you going?"

She told him.

"At least take someone with you."

A thought occurred to her. "I'll give my sister-in-law, Gina, a call. She can give me Catelyn's number." Ian was married to Gina Santino. Gina's sister, Catelyn, was a homicide detective with the Spartanburg County police department.

"Good thinking."

Nick came down the stairs looking like he hadn't slept. He probably hadn't. "Good morning, Nick." She walked over to him and placed a hand on his arm. "Have you decided what you're going to do?"

His warm hand reached up and squeezed her fingers. In spite of the situation, she shivered. She pulled her hand away. He sighed and said, "I'm not sure yet. I'm going to the courthouse. That was Wayne. He and I have something we need to discuss."

"All right, I'll meet you there. I've got a little errand to run."

He frowned. "What kind of errand?"

She frowned and bit her lip. He wanted to talk to Wayne. That wasn't what she wanted to hear. Would warning him away from the man do any good? "I'm investigating that hunch I was telling you about." One that involved his friends.

Nick glanced at his watch. "And you still won't tell me?"

She paused, thought about it, then sighed. "I won't be long, I promise. I'll just be about fifteen minutes behind you and Mason. Lindsey is going to be covered by one of the FBI agents, so everything is all set, okay?"

He nodded, but and the look in his eyes said he didn't like the fact that she wasn't telling him everything. Still, if she was wrong, he didn't need to know what she was thinking.

If she was right... Well, he would find out eventually.

But should she tell him now? After all, it was his nephew who was missing. And he was headed to the courthouse, to seek out the very man she suspected knew a lot more than he was telling.

She hesitated, then decided she couldn't walk out of the

door and send him to the courthouse unarmed. "Do me a favor and stay away from Wayne Thomas, will you?"

Pulling up short, Nick frowned at her. "Wayne? Why?"

"He's my hunch."

Nick laughed. "You're way off there, Carly. Wayne's my best friend and has been for years. He loves Christopher and Lindsey almost as much as I do. He just called, in fact, to see if there was any news." Sobering, he added, "And remember, one of the people snatched was his daughter. You need to look elsewhere."

"That's why I didn't want to say anything. I'm not sure, and I want to check it out."

"You're wasting your time, Carly," he insisted. "Leave Wayne out of this."

"We've got to cover all the angles, remember?"

Nick's nostrils flared. "I'm telling you that's one angle you need to leave alone."

Carly's shoulders stiffened. "Are you telling me how to do my job?"

"I'm telling you that you're wrong, and I want you to leave it alone. You looked into Debbie and Wayne already, and they turned up clean except for Debbie's former connection to a de Lugo relative. A mistake she corrected as soon as she figured out he wasn't a straight-up guy. Now you want to continue to investigate the man who stood by me when my wife died, who encouraged me to move to Spartanburg to give the kids a new start? A man I trust with my life?"

By the end of his outburst, his chest heaved, his anger crystal-clear.

Hurt at his lack of trust in her skills and her intuition, her desire to do everything in her power to find Christopher, she simply sighed and said, "Yeah. And while you think it's a mistake, I think I'm doing the right thing. If I'm wrong, I'll apologize. But this is my job, so let me do it."

Nick simply glared at her for a few seconds, then spun on his heel to exit the room.

Heart aching at his obvious distress, she wondered if she should just drop it. But the intuition he'd shot down in his tirade raised its head and demanded action.

She pulled out her cell phone and placed a call to her boss, explaining the situation. He said he'd have backup headed her way, but gave her permission to carry out her plan. And to use Catelyn in it.

Five minutes later, she'd acquired a vehicle via one of the agents and set off on her "errand." Five minutes after that, she had Catelyn on the phone.

"Can you meet me at this address?" Carly rattled it off.

"Um. Yeah. I'm on the tail end of a report, but I can head that way in about three minutes."

"Great." Excitement pounded through her at the thought of finding Christopher—and Debbie. "Oh, and can you call the alarm-system company and tell them whatever you have to to get it shut off? I want the element of surprise on my side. Also, bring backup with you. If I'm right, we're going to need it."

"Okay, I can do that."

"And wait outside the gate until I tell you to come in."

"O-kay." Catelyn drew the word out. A slight pause. "You are going to explain all this to me at some point, right?"

"Yes, I promise. I just need you as backup in case I'm right—and I'm pretty sure I am."

Ten minutes later, her fingers clutched the steering wheel as she made her way to the property. Her one issue was the gate. She didn't want to announce her presence until she was ready, so she had to figure how to get in without anyone spotting her. She had the right to enter, as she had probable cause to suspect someone was in danger.

If she was wrong, she'd face the consequences like a big girl.

The wrought-iron gate came into view, and Carly parked off the road to the side. She'd also have to be careful of any security cameras. If they were on a separate system than the alarm system, they would still be active.

Five minutes later, Catelyn pulled up. Carly's brother, Ian, sat in the passenger seat.

Climbing out of the vehicle, Carly greeted her brother with a hug and a promise to catch up later, then said to Catelyn, "I need to hurry. Mason is at the courthouse with Nick, and I promised I'd be right behind them."

"What happens if you run into trouble? How will I know?"

"She won't run into any trouble," Ian growled. "I'll be right behind her."

Carly lasered her brother with a glare. "You will not." Then she softened. "But I'm glad you're part of my backup. You'll have to tell me how that happened later. As for how you'll know if I'm in trouble..." She thought about it. "Call me in fifteen minutes. I have my phone on vibrate. If I don't answer, send in reinforcements."

"Got it."

Carly left Catelyn, Ian and the other arriving officers and made a slow tour of the perimeter of the fence. The house sat at the top of horseshoe-shaped drive. Thankfully, there weren't any dogs.

Carly finally found a spot where she could safely scale the fence. The back of the house nudged up against the woods. Several cut trees lay against the fence as though waiting to be hauled off.

Perfect.

Placing one foot on the wood, she carefully launched herself up and over the fence. Skirting the cameras she noticed on each corner of the house just in case, she made her way to the nearest window. The drapes had been drawn, but there was a crack, and she could see in. The den was empty, but the light was on.

Slowly, she moved toward the next window. The kitchen.

The parted blinds allowed her a partial view of the breakfast table. An older lady sat at one end, but she couldn't see if anyone occupied the chair at the other. Then a small hand reached for a piece of toast, and Carly caught her breath. Christopher.

She was right. But who was with him?

A cold, hard object pressed against the back of her head, and she froze.

"Well, well, so you aren't as dumb as I figured."

"And you, Debbie Thomas, deserve an Oscar."

FOURTEEN

Nicholas rode in silence to the courthouse. Two police cars followed behind, one ahead. They weren't taking any chances making sure he got there in one piece. A fact he appreciated, but he couldn't help wondering what Carly was up to. She'd asked him to stay away from Wayne.

A ridiculous request in his opinion, but now that he was thinking clearly, he was able to wonder what kind of information she had that she needed to check out.

He gave himself a mental slap. If he hadn't reacted so strongly, so emotionally, he might have asked her what kind of evidence she had that made her suspect Wayne. And now she was going off and checking something out.

She would possibly be in danger.

His heart ached at the thought of her being hurt. The fact that he could lose her sent stabs of fear through him, and he realized with some amount of shock that losing her might be something he wouldn't be able to recover from.

He also realized he was thinking of a future with Carly—and with Christopher. He couldn't think of one without the boy. The lump that had been in his throat ever since he'd learned of Christopher's disappearance seemed to swell, blocking his air.

He gasped, and Mason looked at him. "Are you all right?"

Nick shut his eyes for a moment and swallowed, trying to force the lump down. It didn't go far. "Just thinking about Christopher."

Understanding flashed on the man's face. "Yeah."

"Do you know what Carly found out?"

"No, she didn't tell me. Said if she was wrong she just wanted to let it drop."

"I should have asked her why she suspects Wayne. Instead, I went off on her. But she's wrong," Nick insisted. "Wayne wouldn't have anything to do with that. I mean, why kidnap his own daughter? It doesn't make sense." He frowned. "Still, if Carly suspects Wayne, isn't that dangerous, investigating that on her own?"

Mason gave a laugh. "Yes, but that's Carly." Compassion lit his gaze as he saw the worried expression on Nick's face. "She'll be careful, and she won't be alone. She's got backup."

"So, she does this kind of thing on a regular basis?" He could lose her.

The shaft of pain that bolted through him stunned him.

Mason sighed. "Look, Nick. Carly is good at her job. Yeah, she had a rough spot for a while when Hank was killed, but she doesn't have a death wish. She's careful and she's good. She'll be fine."

Nick wanted to believe that. With everything in him, he did. But could he?

He had to. Just like he'd entrusted Christopher into God's capable and loving hands, he realized he had to do the same with Carly.

Please, Lord, watch over her....

And then there was the trial. The heaviness he'd carried

on his shoulders since learning of Christopher's disappearance seemed to triple in weight.

Oh, God, I need Your help, Your guidance. Show me what to do today. I still don't know whether to recuse myself or sit on the trial. I know You're a God of justice, and I feel like You've placed me where I am today to help carry out that justice...but, God...Christopher. Can I really follow through with this knowing they'll kill him?

And with a clarity that startled him, he knew he couldn't.

I can't do it, God. I can't. If I sit on that trial and they find Christopher's body, how would I live with myself? I would feel like a murderer. How can You ask me to do this?

The prayer was silent, but the cry echoed in his heart and mind like a shout over the Grand Canyon. For the first time, real anger stirred past the fear, and Nick had to exert serious effort to tamp it down, reminding himself of God's promises, His steadfast love, His plans known only to Him.

"We're here."

Mason's voice cut into his prayers. Taking a deep breath, Nick waited for the marshal to come around and open his door. Police cars waited on either side of him.

They were waiting for him to exit the car so they could safely escort him into the building. The darkness of the parking garage pressed in on him. It angered him that he felt like he needed to look behind every car and cement pillar to make sure no one lurked, ready to shoot or jump out at him.

Squaring his shoulders, he released his seat belt and patted the BlackBerry that had been returned to him. Protection would continue throughout the trial and as long as the threat existed. He hoped that threat would be nonexistent after today.

Please, God, tell me what to do. I can't put Christopher on the line. How can You?

"For I know the plans I have for you. Plans to prosper you, not to harm you…." He whispered the verse out loud.

Mason opened the door, and Nick stepped out. His phone vibrated, and he saw that Wayne was calling.

Following Mason as the man crossed the parking garage toward the elevator, Nick noticed two police officers following close behind.

He hesitated, Carly's words ringing in his ears. Then he cleared his throat and answered his phone, "Hello?"

"So, what's the verdict? Are you going to do the smart thing and let me preside over this trial? I'm here and ready to step in."

Nick froze. *Are you going to do the smart thing? Are you going to do the smart thing? Are you going…*

His breath left him.

"Nick? Nick? Are you all right? You need to keep moving. You can't just stand here in the garage. It's not safe." Mason's voice seemed to come from the end of a long tunnel. Nick blinked, fury rising up in him. He took a deep breath.

"I'm fine." He cleared his throat. "Uh, Wayne, let's talk."

"I'm in my chambers."

"I'll be there in less than a minute."

Nick's footsteps echoed back at him as he hurried down the hall, Mason trailing behind him. He ignored the man's command to slow down. Rage thundered through him. He had to know…

Rounding the corner, a sudden thought occurred to him,

and he did a one-eighty. Mason pounded along beside him. "What are you doing, Nick?"

"I need to get something from my office."

"All right. But I can tell. You're up to something."

"I need to talk to someone."

Nick knew his words were clipped. He wasn't keeping Mason in the dark on purpose; he just wasn't finished processing what he suspected.

Without stopping, he shoved open the door to his chambers and waved Jean down as she popped to her feet.

"Good morning, Nick."

"Morning." Never breaking stride, he hit the door to his inner chambers. He went straight to his desk, yanked open the top drawer to his right and pulled out what he'd come for. He slipped the device into his suit coat pocket and whirled back for the exit.

Mason once again shadowed Nick's footsteps. "Nick, if you're going to see Wayne, I need to ask that you not do that. Not until Carly finishes looking into whatever it is she's looking into."

"I don't have time to wait on her. I'm going to get to the bottom of this myself."

Mason placed a hand on Nick's shoulder and brought him to a halt. Narrow-eyed, the marshal told him, "I can't let you do that."

"You can't stop me."

"It might not be safe."

"I'm willing to take that chance. You don't have to come with me. In fact, as of this moment, you're off the case."

Mason snorted. "Right. If you're dead set on doing this, you'll need someone to have your back."

Nick stopped, looked the officer in the eye. "Thank you."

The marshal's shoulders lifted in a resigned shrug,

and Nick felt a twinge of guilt. Was he putting Mason in danger? He couldn't do that.

"No. If I'm acting irresponsibly, I can't put you in harm's way. You stay out here."

A laugh erupted from Mason. "As if. To borrow your line, you can't stop me from going with you."

Nick gave a short nod but was deeply appreciative of Mason's willingness to be so diligent in his job. He whispered a prayer for his safety.

Jaw set with purpose, he walked over one hall and turned left. At the first door on the right, he raised his fist and knocked.

The door opened, and Wayne Thomas stood there in his judicial robe, his left hand completing the task of zipping it.

"May we come in?"

"Sure, but make it quick, I have a trial starting shortly."

"Tell them it's going to be delayed for a bit. We have to talk." Nick bit down hard on his tongue to keep from hurling the words his brain wanted him to speak.

Wayne's eyes grew wary. "What's this all about?"

Mason stepped to the side, eyes watchful. "Nick? You want to fill me in on what you're doing?"

"I'm exposing the man who had my nephew kidnapped."

Mason tensed, and his eyes darted to Judge Wayne Thomas. "Come on, Nick, you can't just throw that out without some serious evidence to back it up."

Nostrils flaring, Wayne glared at Nick. "Exactly. After all the years of friendship, working together, getting each other through the lousy times in our lives, you would accuse me of having something to do with Christopher's disappearance?"

Nick felt his phone vibrate. He ignored it. "I just put it all together."

Wayne crossed to his desk, settled into his chair and laced his fingers across his stomach. Disdain dripped from him. Not the emotion Nick had been hoping for. Hurt or shock, maybe even disbelief are what he'd wanted to see on his friend's face when Nick dropped his bombshell.

Grief ripped through him. The disdain said it all. "Why, Wayne?"

The man's hand flashed like lightning, and before Nick could blink, he was staring at the wrong end of a serious weapon—complete with silencer. Mason moved almost as fast, but before his hand could pull his own gun, a slight pop sounded and the marshal dropped to the floor, a hole in his chest and the red stain spreading fast. "Ah…"

A phone rang, and Nick raced to the fallen marshal. Ignoring the ringing phone and Wayne's orders to leave the man alone, he grabbed the clean handkerchief he'd put in his pocket that morning and held it against Mason's chest. "Hang on, Mason. We're going to get out of this." He couldn't tell exactly how badly the man was hit. Rage hit him—anger and extreme guilt at himself for putting Mason in danger, and bitter fury at the man who'd done so many despicable acts. He looked at Wayne. "Are you crazy?"

Wayne held the gun on Nick. "No. Tired. And maybe a little desperate."

"Desperate? You just shot a man! A U.S. Marshal! He needs an ambulance."

"It's too late to worry about him. The people I work for want me on the de Lugo trial, and that's the way it's going to play out. I was hoping you would do the smart thing and recuse yourself, but your lousy integrity just wouldn't let you do it, would it?" He sighed. "I was afraid of that."

Cold fear and a fury like he'd never felt before swept over Nick, blinding him for a moment. Somewhere in the back of his mind, he knew he had to keep his cool or he was a dead man. And if he died, where did that leave Christopher and Lindsey? He whispered a quick, desperate prayer, then looked down at the unconscious man whose blood now covered his hands. And now Mason was hurt because of him.

Taking a deep breath, Nick faced the man he thought he could trust with his life. The man who would gain custody of Lindsey and Christopher should anything happen to Nick. His stomach turned at the thought.

There was no way he could let that happen.

"You won't get away with this, Wayne."

Wayne smirked. "Oh, don't be so clichéd. Of course I will."

"You're in de Lugo's pocket. That trial two years ago, the one that I passed over to you, the defendants were connected to the de Lugo family, weren't they?"

"Yes."

Pain nearly shattered him. Taking a deep breath, he asked, "So is Debbie in this with you?"

"Of course. I couldn't have done it without her."

"She let you know where we were the whole time, didn't she?"

"Yes. All we had to do was track her cell phone. Now, we're going to move out of here and down the hall like everything is just fine."

"I'm not going anywhere. Where's Christopher?"

"Christopher is just fine. A very happy little boy who loves my daughter like his own mother."

Nick's fingers curled into fists, and he wanted nothing more than to smash the man's face. *God help me*. With effort, he pulled in another calming breath, ordering himself to keep calm. He couldn't act on impulse. "Speaking of Christopher's mother, my sister—you had something to do with her death, didn't you?"

Surprise lifted Wayne's brow. He paused, still standing behind his desk. "Now, what would make you ask that?"

"Because two years ago, right before she died, when we were still working together in Myrtle Beach, you started pressuring me to recuse myself and hand a specific trial over to you. I refused. Your words, 'Are you going to do the smart thing and let me take care of it?' were the same as the ones you said to me while I was on the way up here. I refused back then, and my wife and sister died in a one-car 'accident.' I refused this time, and my life is threatened and my nephew kidnapped."

"Could have just been a coincidence. But you're right—it wasn't. Still, I don't have time to explain." Wayne waved the gun then pointed it back at Nick. "Now, we need to get going. I gave my secretary the day off because I figured I might need to take some drastic action. I didn't picture it quite like this, however. Now, I've got business to take care of." He looked down at Mason. "And I've got to get that cleaned up. Help me get him hidden in the bathroom."

"Help you? I don't think so. We're not doing anything until you explain yourself. You're admitting you had my wife and sister killed?"

Sickness almost overcame Nick. How had a man he'd loved and trusted become so warped and twisted?

Wayne pointed the gun at the wounded man and growled. "Yes. Now move him, or I'll put another bullet in him. This time I'll aim for his head."

Right now, Mason was still alive. Barely, but he seemed to be hanging on. If Nick refused, a bullet to the head would end all hope of Mason surviving.

Feeling helpless and hating it intensely, Nick shot Wayne

a glare. Offering a silent plea for forgiveness from Mason, Nick reached down and slid his hands under the marshal's armpits. Being as gentle as possible, trying not to do any more damage, he pulled Mason inch by inch into the bathroom.

He laid him on the rug in front of the shower. The wound had opened up and was bleeding again due to the movement. Nick laid two fingers against the man's throat. His pulse was slow and thready. Mason needed help, and he needed it fast. Whispering a prayer over the marshal he'd come to respect and consider a friend, Nick left him in the hands of God.

With a wary eye on Wayne—once his closest friend—Nick stepped out of the bathroom.

"Shut the door."

Nick didn't bother arguing. He shut it.

When Wayne grabbed the Do Not Disturb sign, Nick knew that once the man hung it on the outer chamber door, no one would dare enter. Mason would lie there and bleed to death while Wayne took care of Nick elsewhere. But he needed Nick alive for now. Nick still hadn't recused himself from the case.

Of course, if he were dead it wouldn't be an issue. But then again, the trial might be postponed and there would always be the chance that another judge other than Wayne would be appointed to it. If Nick recused himself, he could recommend that Wayne replace him and no one would think anything of it.

"Why not just shoot me here?"

"Don't play dumb. You know why." Wayne smirked. "Plus, it's too much trouble to clean up two dead bodies. One, I might get away with, but two? I don't think so."

Nick dug in his heels. "I'm not budging. Tell me why you killed Miriam and my sister."

A disgruntled sigh blew from the judge. "It wasn't supposed to be them. It was supposed to be you. Miriam was driving your car." He shook his head as though disgusted. "I figured we'd have to try again. However, after their deaths you did us a huge favor. You fell apart, and we didn't have to worry about you for a while."

It was all Nick could do to contain himself from launching across the desk and strangling the man. However, the gun held in Wayne's very steady hand made him pause and reconsider.

Then Wayne came from behind the desk and said, "Walk toward the door."

Stubbornly, Nick held his ground.

Wayne eyed him. "Do it, or I'll make one call and have Christopher killed."

The breath left Nick's lungs. Hard brown eyes stared back at him. No remorse, no concern, no sign of the years of friendship. Just a flat, hard stare.

When he found his voice, Nick said, "You know, I was real close to recusing myself from the trial when the incident with the two marshals happened and I thought I'd lost Christopher and Lindsey forever. Then Lindsey begged me not to."

Wayne frowned and gave an impatient sigh. "I really don't care."

Ignoring the not-so-subtle hint, Nick continued, "She said she wanted the person to pay, that we couldn't let ourselves be frightened by the bad people in the world. She also said she didn't want me to give the trial to you because the last time you took a trial I was supposed to sit on, the bad people got off."

Wayne snorted. "Are you going somewhere with this?"

"I'm just amazed she saw something in you that I never

noticed. I even excused it, saying that the officers had probably messed up and you had no choice."

"Indeed, those officers did mess up, thankfully. I didn't even have to cover anything up that time."

"That time? How many other times have there been, Wayne? And why?"

"It doesn't matter. And I'm getting really sick of repeating myself. Let's go. Now, or Christopher dies."

Nick turned toward the door and felt the gun touch the middle of his back.

FIFTEEN

Carly didn't move as the gun pressed harder into her skull. "Debbie, what are you doing? Is Christopher all right?"

"Christopher is fine. No thanks to you or his uncle, who, by the way, could have avoided all this if he'd just recused himself and let my father take over. But no, Mr. Goody Two-Shoes had to let his integrity get in the way of being smart." Disgust curled in her voice. "Now, I want you take your gun out of your shoulder holster and put it on the ground. Understand?"

"All right. Then what?"

"Just do it."

Carly reached ever so slowly toward her gun, her right arm crossing over to pull the weapon from its resting place under her left arm. For a second, she considered a self-defense move, but when Debbie warned, "Don't try anything funny. I'll pull this trigger so fast, you'll be dead before you can regret it."

Deciding it might be best to go along with Debbie for the moment, Carly ignored her impulse to act.

Debbie ordered, "Now get inside. I've got to figure out what to do with you. Where to…hide you."

A chill swept over Carly at the slight pause in the last part of that sentence.

"You know, if you kill me, it's going to be pretty hard to hide the fact. A lot of people know where I am."

A pause. "Then I'll have to hurry and come up with a plan, won't I? Plus, I'll have some help."

"Like Ben McCann? The cop who was bought off and helped you snatch Christopher?"

A swift indrawn breath echoed behind her.

"You leave Ben out of this. He's just an innocent bystander who got in the way that day."

"Why should I leave him out of it? He failed to keep Christopher from being snatched right under his nose. He was in it with you—not so innocent if you ask…" Her voice trailed off as a thought occurred to her. "Wait a minute. There wasn't anyone else involved, was there? We didn't miss seeing someone cross the open space between the building and the trees. Because no one crossed it, did they? You hit Ben—or Ben beat himself up—and you just hopped in the car and drove off."

"Like I said, you're not as dumb as you look. Yes, Ben knocked his head against the cabinet." She grimaced. "He did it really hard, too."

"Hard enough to kill himself."

Debbie bit her lip, shock contorting her face at the blunt statement. Carly picked up on that. "Did Ben mean something to you, Debbie?"

"Ben's dead?"

"He died from bleeding to the brain. A stroke, they said."

The gun wavered, and Carly wanted to snatch the moment, rush the woman and knock the weapon from her hand.

Just as she was about to move, Debbie tightened her grip and Carly flinched, expecting to hear the sharp snap of the gun and feel the painful hit of the bullet.

Neither happened.

Tears filled Debbie's eyes, and she quickly wiped them away. "Well, he was stupid anyway. Such an easy target. He couldn't think for himself." Her chin lifted, and the hardness returned to her eyes.

She waved her weapon in the air, and Carly jerked again, ready to duck or run in order to avoid being shot. Then Debbie smirked, her tears for the dead man gone. "No, he didn't mean anything to me. He thought he did, but I was just leading him on to get him to do what we needed him to do. And he did it. That's all that matters."

Carly gestured to the bandage on Debbie's left hand. "How did you do that?"

"Got in a hurry and slammed the door on it."

"So, Ben beat himself up and you just popped Christopher in the car and took off."

"Exactly."

"That was some pretty fancy driving."

"I know."

"And then you ditched the car."

"Right. I figured there would be some way to track it so I simply parked it—right where you probably found it—and Chris*tina* and her *daddy* hopped on a bus."

"You were prepared the whole time. With disguises and everything." Of course, they hadn't monitored what Debbie had packed. "You took the outfit from Christopher's suitcase, didn't you?"

"Yes, and the inhaler from the bathroom."

"That's what tipped me off."

Debbie's right brow lifted. "What?"

"You were the only one with access. You were the only one that made any sense. It was so organized, so planned." She sighed. "When you didn't bother to grab the inhaler from the counter in our rush to leave the safe house, it was because you didn't need it. You already had one." Carly clicked her tongue. "Very obvious."

Anger twisted the woman's features. "Well, it couldn't have been too obvious, as it took you this long to figure it out."

Carly ignored the insult. "So, is your father involved in all of this, too?"

"Of course. Who do you think recruited me?"

Sickness swirled in Carly's stomach. *Oh, Nick, how betrayed you're going to feel.*

If he lived long enough to feel it. "Nick's on his way to the courthouse now. What is your father going to do when Nick doesn't recuse himself?"

"I'm not worried about that. Right now I've got to take care of you. Now, move toward the door."

Carly did as ordered but wanted to keep the woman talking. The more she talked, the more time Carly had to think of a way out of this. She had to get to the courthouse to warn Nicholas.

She moved toward the door, her arms held up and away from her sides. *Come on, Catelyn, be early. Call me.*

Fortunately, she'd tucked her cell phone into the back pocket of her jeans. She knew for a fact if she'd had it clipped to her belt like she normally did, Debbie would have had her toss that, too. But she hadn't wanted to take a chance on snagging it on the fence when she'd climbed over, so she'd transferred it.

With the gun pressed against her head, Carly moved carefully, not wanting to cause Debbie to trip on anything and accidentally pull the trigger. Nerves tight, Carly focused on getting in the house to see if she could spot Christopher. "You might want to point that gun elsewhere. If it goes off, it's going to be awfully messy. How would you explain it?"

A low chuckle came from behind her. "I'm not worried about it. I've been handling guns since I was a teen and Daddy took me to the range."

Great. But it was good information to have. At least she knew Debbie would hit what she shot at.

Debbie shoved the door open and gave Carly a rough push into the foyer. "Where are your handcuffs?"

"I left them in the car." And she had. She hadn't wanted to take a chance on them jingling. Not that it mattered now. "How did you know I was out there?"

"The security camera mounted on the tree in the woods. I watched you climb over the fence."

"Ah. Missed that one."

"That's why it's there."

"Right." Carly glanced around, looking for any sign of the boy. "Where's Christopher?"

"None of your business. Now sit." Another shove in the small of her back sent her forward toward the armchair near the fireplace.

Carly sat. "Now what? Are you going to kill me?"

"We're going to wait."

"For what? Orders? Yeah, you're good at following Daddy's orders, aren't you, Debbie? Why don't you start thinking for yourself and realize you won't get away with this?"

With a growl, Debbie stalked toward her and back-handed her with the barrel of the gun. Carly cried out at the slash of pain and nearly fell from the chair.

Inwardly, she felt a surge of satisfaction. So, the little nanny had a bit of a temper. Somehow she had to find a way to use that. Ignoring the throbbing just over her right eye, she felt warm wetness slide down the side of her face. A drop of blood dripped from her chin to land on her jeans-clad thigh.

Her phone vibrated, and she breathed a sigh of relief.

Hopefully, help would arrive before Debbie decided to kill her—or received the order to do so. "How are you going to hold me here? You've got no handcuffs. You can't leave me to get some rope.... Come on, Debbie, give it up." She really needed to get to the courthouse. Fear for Nick nearly overwhelmed her. But she had to focus on the woman in front of her and pray that God would watch over Nicholas.

Yes, pray.

So she did. With her eyes open, searching for the slightest drop in Debbie's guard. She had no doubt the opportunity would present itself, but would it be in time to get to Nick?

And she still had to find Christopher.

Debbie hissed. "How did you put it all together? I was so careful, played the part so well. How did you know to come here?"

"Like I said, it was obvious. You left clues all over the place."

"I did not!" Debbie yelled. Then glanced toward the stairs. A quick glance that didn't give Carly a chance to react. Debbie lowered her voice. "I didn't."

"You dropped your cell phone in the garage of the second safe house."

"So what? I was kidnapped. What's so special about finding a phone I dropped in a struggle?"

"I'd taken the phone from you and put it in the kitchen drawer, remember? That's why you were so intent on getting stuff from the kitchen as we were all in a hurry to get out of the house. Your entire focus was on getting that phone, or your connection to your partner would be cut off."

"Yes," she hissed, "that's right. And before you ask, I

messed with the stove while you were sleeping and Mason was doing his patrol of the grounds."

Stunned, Carly just stared at her. "But you could have killed yourself as well as everyone else in the house. The kids…"

Debbie scowled. "I was going to save them." She tapped her chest. "I was going to be the hero. I was about to tell Nick to get away from the stove when you opened your big mouth." A sneer curled her lip. "Then I just had to be meek little Debbie and play along."

Desperate to get away and find Christopher so she could warn Nicholas, Carly's mind formed and rejected plan after plan, her mind clicking through them at warp speed. *God, please…*

"Who was the older lady I saw at the kitchen table?"

"My grandmother. Now shut up." Uncertainty flickered across Debbie's face for the first time since she'd forced Carly into the house. "Okay, here's the plan. I'm going to lock you in the storage room, and then I'll ask Daddy what he wants to do with you when he gets home. Now, get up slowly and walk toward the kitchen. You know which way it is, since you decided to snoop at the window."

Where was Catelyn? Or Ian?

A thump sounded from overhead, and both women looked up. Carly snatched the chance and dove at Debbie, clipping her around her legs. With a screech, Debbie went down, and the gun went flying.

A door slammed open and someone yelled, "Freeze! Police!"

Debbie tried to scramble away from Carly's grip on her ankle, but Carly wasn't letting go. She yanked hard, and Debbie went flat on her stomach again.

Carly knew the woman was going after the gun. She'd heard it skitter across the hardwood floors. That meant it had flown out of Debbie's hand hard enough to bypass the large area rug they were now doing battle on.

Debbie kicked out with her other foot, and Carly felt pain lance her from her hand to her arm. Heart thumping, adrenaline surging, Carly yelled, "Don't shoot her!"

Finally gaining some momentum against the writhing woman, Carly hefted herself to her knees and grabbed Debbie's flailing arm. The strength Debbie displayed surprised her, and she fought to get a knee in her lower back. "Debbie, stop fighting. Give it up!"

"No! No! You can't do this!"

Someone slapped a pair of handcuffs in Carly's hand, and she twisted Debbie's arm behind her back. Quickly, she snapped the cuff on. Vaguely, she registered Catelyn had a grip on Debbie's legs and someone else was pulling Debbie's other arm back so Carly could enclose the cuff around it.

It was done. Ian pointed a gun at the nanny as officers swarmed the rest of the house.

Debbie was subdued, crying her misery into the floor.

Carly looked up at Catelyn. "What took you so long?"

"We had to figure out how to get past the stupid gate without setting off all kinds of alarms. This place has more booby traps than Fort Knox." She grunted. "Your Ranger brother here came in mighty handy."

"Yes, he can do that occasionally," she grunted as she hauled herself to her feet. The room spun for a second, and someone gripped her arm.

"Are you okay?" Ian asked.

Carly looked up. "I'll be fine. Just a little dizzy from the knock on the head." He pressed a cloth to it, and she asked, "How did you get involved in all of this anyway?"

"I was in the neighborhood and thought I'd stop by." His

handsome face frowned at her. "We need to get someone to look at that head of yours."

She waved a hand of dismissal and said, "I'm fine. I need to call Nick and warn him about Debbie's father."

She rattled off the number for Catelyn, who punched it into her phone even as the woman asked, "So, you were right about everything, huh?"

"Yeah. Unfortunately. Now we just need to find Christopher."

"Miss Carly!"

Carly spun to see Debbie's grandmother standing in the doorway flanked by two police officers.

And Christopher launching himself at her.

She caught him up in a hug and struggled not to keel over between the quivering muscles and the pounding head. But the feel of his little warm body against hers made her want to weep in relief—and gratitude.

"Thank You, God," she whispered against his ear. To Christopher she said, "I'm so glad you like to jump on beds."

He grinned. "I didn't have any beanbags, so I put the pillows on the floor and jumped. I landed kinda hard, though, and it made a loud noise. Did you hear it?"

"Boy, did I ever." She gathered his little face in her hands and asked, "Did Debbie hurt you, Christopher?"

He frowned and looked past her at the cuffed woman who now sat in a zombielike state on the floor, hands bound behind her. "No. But she wouldn't let me call Uncle Nick, and that made me mad. She said Uncle Nick was busy, and I had to stay with her until he was done. I asked why couldn't Lindsey come, too, and she said 'cuz Lindsey didn't want to. Miss Carly, why is your head bleeding?"

Carly gave him another hug and checked his breathing. No wheezing. Apparently, he'd received good care while at the Thomas home and suffered no lasting effects from his kidnapping. "It's a long story, Christopher. Let's talk about it later."

"I can't get Nicholas on his phone," Catelyn said, interrupting them and drawing Carly's attention back to the situation.

"Try Mason." She gave her that number while Christopher moved his choke hold from Carly's neck to her waist.

"No answer, Carly." Catelyn's brows met above the bridge of her nose. "This isn't good."

Real fear blossomed in Carly's midsection. She set Christopher on his feet and looked him in the eye. "Christopher, I want you to go with these nice policemen here, okay? I've got to go find your uncle and let him know you're okay."

"I want to go with you." He wrapped an arm around her leg and looked up at her, imploring her with his gold-green eyes that looked so much like his uncle's.

"Chris…"

His lower lip quivered. "Please?"

Carly shot a desperate look toward Catelyn. "Bring him with you to the courthouse, okay? When everything is… taken care of, Nick will want to see him immediately. Can we do that?"

"Sure."

Carly looked at Christopher. "That's the best I can do, kiddo."

"Okay. I'll take it."

He sounded so old and resigned, Carly wanted to laugh. But she didn't have time. Looking at Ian, she asked, "Are you here to help or look pretty?"

"Can't I do both?"

"Call for backup at the courthouse and tell them I'm on

my way." It would be one thing she wouldn't have to do as she raced from the Thomas home to the courthouse. She had to find Nick and Mason as soon as possible.

Two men who should be answering their phones and weren't.

SIXTEEN

Nick took another step toward the door then turned back. Wayne shoved him, and he pretended to stumble, going to his knees. He knew Carly would be looking for him at some point. Buying time was the best idea he could come up with. Or opening up a chance to jump Wayne.

Not having to feign anger, Nick glared at his betrayer and said, "If you want me to walk, I suggest you not be so physical."

Fury glistened down at him in the other man's eyes. "Get up, you idiot, and walk to the door. Any more funny stuff and I guess I'll have to clean up two bodies after all."

Nick hauled himself to his feet, remembered Mason's still form and agonized that he wasn't able to help him more. He held out a beseeching hand. "Come on, Wayne, think of our history." He refused to think about the fact that the man had had a hand in the murder of his wife and sister. All he was interested in now was getting Wayne to either give it up—or hope Carly showed up soon.

The gun lifted to point at his nose. "Go."

Time was up. He had no choice. Without another thought, Nick shot out a hand and knocked the gun to the side, away from his face.

Wayne cursed and brought the gun around, catching Nick on the side of the head.

His world spun and all went dark for a brief moment as he sank back to his knees. This time for real. Then Wayne had him by the back of his collar, jerking him to his feet.

With a shove, Wayne slammed him against the wall and growled, "You just signed Christopher's death warrant. Now open that door."

Head throbbing, heart pounding, Nick's fury rose up in him to mammoth heights, but he knew jumping Wayne again was out of the question. Wayne was just too careful about leaving himself open. He'd be extra vigilant now.

"Fine." *Oh, God, I failed. Please rescue Christopher.*

Nick reached for the doorknob and twisted.

Finally, Carly arrived at the courthouse. Not wanting to tip Wayne off that they were on to him, they'd simply had security shut off all traffic outside Nick and Wayne's chambers. A SWAT team was on alert and ready for action should it be needed. An officer reported the blinds on both judges' chambers were drawn and closed. The officer couldn't see in. They were working on getting a listening device operational.

Carly flashed her badge and made her way inside the building. Two officers flanked her. Two ambulances were on standby and parked at the rear entrance, with more officers on duty in that area.

Her black boots made no sound on the tile floor as she walked down the hall, weapon drawn. The officers behind also held their weapons ready.

At Nick's office, Carly noticed Jean wasn't at her desk. Bypassing the secretary's station, she made her way to the chamber door. She listened, her ear turned in to catch the slightest sound.

Silence.

Carly heard the outer door open, and she spun, gun pointing in that direction. Catelyn entered, stealthily and quietly sliding inside and raising a brow at Carly. Ian followed quickly behind Catelyn.

Carly nodded and motioned them forward. The officers stepped back and Catelyn took her stance on the opposite side of the door. Taking a deep breath, Carly reached out and twisted the knob.

The door flew open, and she darted a glance around the office. Empty.

Lowering her gun, she looked toward the bathroom. The door stood open and she could clearly see it stood empty, too.

Shudders wracked her at the memory of the last time she'd been in here. This time there weren't any snakes. Of the slithering kind. Now she was after a two-legged reptile.

"Clear here," she said. "Let's get to Wayne's office."

They exited the room and hurried down the hall, arriving at Wayne's chambers to find his door closed.

She and Catelyn repeated their actions, each standing on either side of the door. As Carly reached for the knob, it started turning.

Catelyn and Ian jerked back, as did Carly. The door opened. Nick's voice, tense and angry, flowed to her, and relief flooded her. She was in time.

Nick walked through the door, and Carly saw the gun pointed at his back. Almost without thinking, she waited just long enough for Wayne's arm to clear the door and then kicked out in a sweeping motion, catching his wrist. A scream of pain met her ears, and the gun went flying down the hall.

"Freeze, Wayne!"

Nick turned, and his fist shot out to catch the man under the jaw. Carly heard the crack and watched Wayne's head snap back. He stumbled back into the room he'd just exited, disappearing for a brief moment.

She went in after him.

"Carly!"

Nick's harsh shout echoed as she rounded the door-jamb in time to see Wayne dart behind his desk. A drawer opened and slammed shut.

He was going for another weapon.

Ian entered, followed quickly by Catelyn. A bullet slammed into the door above Catelyn's head, and she ducked out. Ian, realizing he had no coverage, bolted back through the door. "You're surrounded, Thomas. Give it up," her brother hollered.

Carly pointed in Wayne's direction and fired. The bullet slammed into the wall, and she saw Wayne's gun lift again.

"Don't try it, Wayne," she called. "You're finished. Cops are crawling all over this building, and Christopher is safe."

A breath whooshed out behind her. She turned. "Nick, get out of here—he's got another weapon." He ignored her, and she noticed he'd taken cover next to the armoire in the corner.

At the crack of the first bullet, she'd darted behind a large, straight-backed chair, the kind of chair someone would have in a nice living room. It hid her fairly well, but she wasn't sure it would stop a bullet, so she wasn't relaxing anytime soon. "Wayne, we've got Debbie in custody. Give it up."

Nick called out, "Always the Boy Scout, huh, Wayne? Two guns? Isn't that a bit of overkill?"

"Shut up, Nick."

Catelyn would have the door blocked. The window behind the desk would afford the SWAT team a good opportunity to take Wayne down should he refuse to surrender.

Only then did she notice the bloodstain on the floor. Nick had been fine.

"Mason? Where's Mason?"

A hard chuckle came from behind the desk. "You need to let me out of here before your friend dies. I can hole up here for a long time."

"Not a chance, Wayne," Carly called. "You should know better than that. If he dies, you'll just go down for his murder." But she wasn't going to let Mason die. What had Wayne done to him? Where was he? Somehow she had to get Wayne to give up or find a way to force his hand.

But how?

Nick spoke up from behind the safety of the armoire. "He's in the bathroom with a gunshot wound, Carly. Wayne's right about one thing—Mason does need immediate medical care."

Carly sucked in a breath. Then time was even more critical than she'd imagined. "Wayne, there's a SWAT team up on the building even as we speak. Even if you get out of the courthouse, where are you going to go?"

Silence from behind the desk. Then, "They can't see me from the window. And even if they could, it's bulletproof glass."

"Yeah, well, even bulletproof glass isn't impenetrable. I think we all had a lesson on that just a couple of days ago," Nick shot back to his former friend.

More silence. A deep sigh came from behind the desk. "For what it's worth, I never wanted to hurt the kids, Nick."

"Sorry, Wayne, it's not worth much. Save it." Nick's

voice could have bent steel. A quick glance at him confirmed the fury in his eyes had reached a new level. Carly lasered him with a don't-you-dare-do-something-stupid look.

He glared right back. But nodded.

Good, he was keeping his cool. More than she might be able to do should their roles be reversed, she admitted grudgingly to herself. Out loud she said, "Wayne, you know they're going to consider Nick and me hostages. Pretty soon a negotiator is going to be here."

No sooner had the words left her lips than the phone on Wayne's desk rang.

Nick waited, tense, every muscle in his body frozen with the need to be ready to act. The phone rang again. "Answer it, Wayne."

"Shut up, Nick. I'm thinking."

Nick wanted to laugh. Instead, he said, "You can't think your way out of this one. It's kind of a no-brainer."

The man didn't respond. Was he considering giving up? Again, the shrill sound of the phone penetrated the thick atmosphere. Then the phone flew over the desk and bounced on the floor, the cord dangling like a kite tail.

Carly's voice sounded. "Yes, we're fine for now." Nick realized she was speaking into her cell phone. When no one answered the landline, whoever was in charge of this situation had opted to call Carly. She continued. "He has a weapon. We have an officer down who needs immediate attention." She went on to summarize their position in short, succinct sentences. "He refuses to answer the phone that is now disabled. I'll keep you apprised of the situation." A pause. "I'll take care of it."

Nick saw her place the phone on the floor beside her. He

wondered if she'd hung up or left the line open. Probably the latter.

Movement from behind Carly's chair pulled his attention to her. She slipped toward the bathroom, her desperate need to check on Mason stamped clearly on her face.

Suddenly a shot rang out and slammed into the wall above her. Nick took a step forward, hand reaching toward her before he realized what he was doing. She ducked back behind the chair, and Nick breathed a sigh of relief.

"Don't shoot," she ordered into her phone. Hopefully, the SWAT team would wait for her signal. "Not smart, Wayne!" she called.

Wayne snarled from behind the safety of his desk, "I told you the only way to save your friend is to get me out of the building."

Thirty seconds passed in silence. Then Carly spoke. "Fine, use me as a hostage. If it means saving Mason's life, I'll do what I can to get you out of here."

"No way, Carly!" Nick protested, his heart thumping double time at what she was suggesting. "Think of another option." He knew that if Wayne got out of the building, away from the cops, the man had the resources to disappear, never to be heard from again.

A fact Wayne was no doubt counting on.

She didn't bother responding, and Nick realized he had no say in the matter. She was letting Wayne think about her offer. The fact that Wayne hadn't laughed in her face greatly concerned him.

Wayne said, "That's the smartest thing I've heard come out of your mouth since I've met you."

Never had Nick wanted to hurt someone so badly. Not normally a violent person, he found himself wanting to pulverize his former friend. "Carly, you can't do this."

"Sure I can." To Wayne, she said, "And I know exactly

how to get you out of here. Hold on and let me make a phone call."

Nick heard her phone chirp twice as she punched in a speed-dial number. Who was she calling?

"Here's the deal. Wayne and I are going to walk out of here. Nick is going to stay with Mason. As soon as we're clear of the room, send the paramedics in."

Not gonna happen, Nick thought, but didn't interrupt. He'd figure out how to get Carly away from Wayne without getting her—or himself—shot.

"As soon as Wayne and I are clear of the building, you send in the paramedics and get Mason to a hospital." She paused. "Yeah, I know it's dangerous, but right now Mason doesn't have time for us to come up with a better plan."

She hung up, dropped her gun to the floor and nudged it up under the chair. Standing, she held her hands above her head and said, "All right, Wayne, let's go." To Nick, she said, "Will you please stay with Mason? I'll be fine, I promise."

"You don't know what this man is capable of, Carly." He couldn't leave her with him. Wayne had shot Mason without blinking. If Carly walked out the door with him, Nick knew without a doubt he'd never see her again.

At least not alive.

Please, Lord, show me what to do.

"In the bathroom, Floyd." Wayne now stood, his gun aimed at Carly.

Nick's mind clicked with possibilities. None of them to his liking. He moved toward the bathroom, wanting to protest, everything in him desperate to protect the woman he now knew he loved—yes, loved.

A roaring sounded in his ears. The world tilted, and Nick lost his breath.

What had he just thought?

Before he had time to actually consider what he'd just admitted, even if it was only to himself, his mind already plotted a plan to help Carly.

Carly stood patiently, eyes never still, while Nick walked to the bathroom. He had to go along for now or else Mason would die.

He might already be dead, but if not, this was his only chance. Nick opened the door and stepped into the bathroom. Turning, his eyes met Carly's. He saw her gaze drop to the officer at his feet. He blinked, wondering what he'd seen flash there for a brief second. Fear? Anger? Helplessness? Rage?

All of the above. Nick knelt beside Mason and placed two fingers on the man's pulse. Almost nonexistent, but still there.

Her eyes rose to meet his once again, and he thought he saw something else.

Love? A silent promise? Definitely something. And a question as to Mason's status.

He mouthed, "Bad, but alive."

Heart pounding, he tried to communicate back to her that he'd be right behind her and Wayne.

She narrowed her eyes and gave a slight shake of her head. He raised a brow in response but didn't change his stance.

With one eye on Nick, Wayne placed the gun in the small of Carly's back and shoved her toward the back door. The exit away from Ian, Catelyn and any backup.

Metal winked at him from under the chair to the left of the bathroom door. As soon as Wayne and Carly were out of the room, Nick went for the gun she'd shoved out of sight. Wayne had been so consumed with getting out of the building that he'd completely forgotten about the weapon.

And her phone, which was still connected to whoever she'd been talking to. Nick swiped that, too.

Cops and paramedics flooded into the room, and, with relief, Nick motioned toward Mason.

In all of the chaos, Nick slipped through the crowd before someone could grab him and headed for the elevator.

He knew exactly how Wayne planned to get out of the building.

Down the stairs, through the basement, to the outside door.

He swept toward the stairwell and shoved the door open. Let it close behind him. Shutting his eyes, he listened.

And heard the faint sound of receding footsteps.

They were going down, just like he figured. Into the phone, he whispered, "Go to the outside basement door. They'll be coming out there."

"Who is this?" the voice barked.

"Judge Nicholas Floyd. I was in the chambers with Deputy Marshal Carly Masterson and Judge Wayne Thomas. He's taken her hostage."

"We know. We heard."

"There's a basement. I heard them in the stairs just a short time ago. I believe he's heading for the basement exit."

"We'll have it covered. Where are you?"

"Following them."

SEVENTEEN

Carly shrugged against the hard hand gripping her upper arm and got nowhere. Sure, she could use some self-defense moves, but there was no guarantee she would get in a good kick before he pulled the trigger.

"So, what are you going to do when you get out of here and after you kill me?"

"Shut up."

"Oh, come on, what's it going to hurt to tell me?" She stumbled down the next flight of stairs and felt the nose of the gun dig into her back. Held at gunpoint twice in one day.

A new record for her.

Wayne stopped her at the door and looked at her. "It won't take much to procure a new identity. Disappearing will be easy."

"That's why you didn't bother to kill Nick back there. You're already planning to go underground."

"Before this day is over, my name will be mud. I'll be a wanted man. Killing Nick's not going to change that."

"Or killing me."

Another pause. "I don't want to kill you." He shoved her toward the door and said, "Open it."

She didn't move.

Another jab with the gun. Hard enough to leave a bruise. She winced.

His voice came closer to her left ear. "Open the door. I don't want to kill you...but I will without hesitating if I need to."

Carly shuddered and placed a hand on the door. She knew he was serious, and for a moment she wondered where she would spend eternity should the unthinkable happen.

She believed in God, had loved Him and wanted His will for her life for a long time. When Hank had died, the faith she'd thought was so strong had crumbled like dust.

And she'd hardened her heart and blamed God.

But Nick hadn't blamed her for the disappearance of Christopher. And he hadn't turned his back on the God who hadn't stopped his wife and sister from dying.

She knew now that God wasn't to blame after all. Death was a consequence of man's disobedience. Maybe Nick was right and bad things just happened because it was a fallen world that had turned its back on God.

Just like she'd done.

Grief hit her all at once, and although she'd made the decision to choose to believe again earlier, the realization of what she'd nearly done to her life, to her spiritual well-being, almost sent her to her knees.

I'm sorry, God. I was wrong. I'm sorry. Please forgive me.

The gun jabbed harder into her lower back, and she gasped. Leaning against the door, she gave it a push. It swung open slightly. Alarm bells rang, but Wayne didn't seem that concerned. Of course, he would have known opening the door would do that. She took a step toward the opening. His grip on her arm yanked her back inside. "What are you doing?"

"Not that way. Nick would have told them to have that door covered. Now we go back up."

A chill swept over Carly. Would the authorities fall for that little trick?

A voice through a bullhorn sounded just over the ringing door. "Wayne Thomas, this is the Spartanburg County Police Department. You are surrounded. Throw your weapon out."

Back up the steps they went, the captain's voice fading as they climbed. "Where are we going?"

"You'll see. Just keep climbing. Two more flights."

"The parking garage."

"You're quick, I'll give you that."

"They'll have cops all over it, Wayne."

"Not the part I'm going for."

What part could he possibly be talking about? She ran through the layout in her mind, but couldn't figure it out. It didn't matter. She didn't plan on letting him get that far anyway.

Now he was behind her. Her mind flashed through possible escape moves. A sound from above reached her ears, and she almost stopped to listen. Instead, she kept going, wondering if someone had figured out what Wayne had planned. She was almost to the parking-garage level. If she was going to act, she needed to do it soon.

"Stop there. Did you hear something?"

"Just you," she lied. There was no way she was going to tip him off if help was just above her.

He snorted. "Right."

Three more steps and she'd be on the landing. But she needed him closer. *Just one more step, Wayne.* "So, are we going to stand here all day?"

"Shut up and let me listen."

"There's nothing up there…"

She felt him move up one more step, shut her mouth and lashed back with her elbow.

A choking, strangling cry met her efforts, and she whirled to see him grab his throat. The gun clattered to the steps and bounced down to the landing below them. Carly held her breath, waiting for the thing to go off and send a bullet flying in a direction she couldn't guess.

When it landed without discharging, she breathed a sigh of relief. She started to go after the weapon, but Wayne was already scrambling back down to retrieve it.

Flight was her only option. Pushing herself up the next flight of stairs, she aimed for where she knew help would be.

"Come back here, Carly! I let your friend live because you said you would get me out of here. Now get back here!"

The man was losing it.

She kept going. Heard him closing in behind her. Her head throbbed in the place where Debbie had pistol-whipped her, but she ignored it and pushed on.

Then Nick was there at the top of the landing.

Wayne thundered behind her.

"Nick, he's got a gun. Get out of sight," she panted.

His eyes flicked over her and revealed pure relief at the fact she was in one piece. Then they hardened and he said, "Be ready to move fast."

"Wha—?"

Then he was a blur, diving past her as Wayne rounded the landing and hit the steps just below her.

Flesh struck flesh and the two men went down, crashing to the floor. Carly blinked and heard a fist connect, followed by a groan and a spurt of blood. Whose, she didn't know, but kept her eye out for the gun.

Nick's arm came back and crashed down. Wayne

hollered and rolled, thumping down the flight of stairs he'd just come up moments before.

Carly raced after him, but once again Nick beat her there. Wayne reached for the gun that had flown from his hand and landed next to the wall.

Nick grabbed for it at the same time and two desperate hands covered it, fought for it.

Wayne pulled Nick off balance, and Nick landed on his former friend with a grunt.

The gun went off next to her left ear, the explosion blasting in the enclosed area. For a brief moment Carly was deafened.

"Nick!" she called.

Blood seeped from between the two men. Fear drummed through her, and with one eye on Wayne, she grabbed for Nick.

He rolled off, fresh blood staining his once pristine white shirt.

At first she thought he was dead but then realized his chest was heaving with the effort to breathe.

Wayne's chest was still. It looked like a bullet had cut a path through his heart that would beat no more. The weapon rested on the floor beside him. She shoved it out of grabbing distance just in case.

A hand on her shoulder made her jump, and she turned to see Nick sitting up and asking her something. She couldn't hear him. Turning her head, she listened with her right ear. "What?"

"Are you okay?"

"Yes," she gulped. "I'm fine. What about you?"

He nodded. "I just want a shower and a change of clothes. And I want to kiss you and tell you everything that's going on inside me."

She gave a small smile. "I think that can be arranged."

* * *

Wayne was dead. Debbie was in custody, and Christopher's grin hadn't left his face since he saw his uncle. When Nick walked out of the courthouse, Catelyn and Ian had been waiting with Christopher. The little boy had thrown himself into his uncle's arms, and Carly had wept at the sweet reunion. Ian had held Carly and let her cry.

Then the two of them got swept along in the aftermath. The paperwork had started for her, and the trial had gotten underway for Nick. She hadn't seen him since, except for brief snatches she managed to get each night on the news as he left the courthouse.

Yesterday, Nick had called and asked her to meet him at Lake Bowen Fish Camp. The trial was over, and de Lugo had been found guilty. Relief like nothing she'd ever felt flowed through her. She'd recused herself from the assignment, as she felt like protecting him had become a conflict of interest for her.

But it was hard putting his safety into other hands. Plus, she missed him.

She loved him.

And she told herself that it wasn't possible. How had she grown to love a man in such a short amount of time?

But there wasn't a doubt in her mind that she did.

And now the case was over. And so was her discontent. Holding onto her anger with Nick and God had just been her way of grieving at first, then quite possibly had become a comfortable habit. But thanks to Nick and his steady faith, Carly had made peace with God and Hank's death. No, it wasn't fair and it made her want to cry from missing him, but acknowledging that it wasn't Nick's fault—or God's—had gone a long way in healing her heart.

She pulled into the parking lot of the restaurant and saw that his car was already there. Joy at the thought of spending time with him lifted her nearly off her feet as she glided through the door. From a booth in the back, he waved at her.

He looked *good*.

As she walked toward him, he stood and hesitantly wrapped her in a hug when she got near enough. She slid her arms around his waist and snuggled next to his heart.

When he pulled away and looked down at her, she could tell he had something pressing on his mind.

"I know it's only been a couple of weeks," Nick said, clearing his throat and shuffling his feet. He slid back into the booth, pulling her in next to him.

"But?"

He took her hand and smiled down at her. "At the safe house, you told me I wasn't crazy when I said I thought we...um..."

"Had feelings for each other?"

He flushed. "Yeah. I'm out of practice with all of this, but I'm...falling in love with you, Carly." He swallowed hard. Her heart fluttered in her chest like a trapped butterfly.

He touched her hand, and she looked up at him. His eyes met hers. "Two weeks ago, when all of the danger was going on and I was going crazy feeling like I was being pulled in a hundred different directions..." He trailed off, and she waited. "You—and God—kept the insanity at bay. You were the calm in my storm. I needed that. I needed you." He traced her eyebrow with his forefinger, and Carly let her eyes drift shut.

Then she opened them and smiled. "I think we did that for each other. I seem to remember a meltdown or two of my own." She paused. "And you turned to the only one that could really do anything about the situation. I loved that about you."

His eyes warmed, and he looked wistful. "Is that all you love about me?"

She felt the heat rise into her cheeks. "No, but I need some feedback here."

"How do you feel about the kids?"

"I'm very fond of them," she said without hesitation. "I would even go so far as to say I've come to love them. We all went through a lot together—that bonds people in a way that just hanging out doesn't compare with. And they're easy kids to love."

He gave a faint smile. "Yes, they squirmed right into my heart the minute I learned of their impending births."

"So, what's the problem?"

Nick blew out a sigh. "I guess I'm afraid."

Not expecting that one, she felt thrown off. "You? Of what?"

Wrapping an arm around her shoulder, he pulled her to him and planted a kiss on top of her head. "That I'll lose you. That the kids will come to love you and look at you as a mother figure, and then—we'll lose you."

Anger stirred, but she pushed it back. She didn't want to be angry. She wanted to know where she stood with him. What he was feeling. "So, you're saying you don't want to take a chance on us?"

"No. That's not what I'm saying. I'm saying I'm scared and I need reassurance—and I'm not sure what to do about that because I've never really been in this situation before. Never really thought it would be an issue. Then you came back into my life, and...here we are."

Carly thought for a moment, wracking her brain for the right words. Sucking in a deep breath then exhaling on a prayer, she said, "Nick, I don't know what to tell you. But do you know what my quiet time this morning was?"

"Quiet time?" Surprise lifted his brow.

"Yes." She nudged him in the rib with an elbow. "Since I've chosen to follow God, I figured I'd better spend time with Him to get reacquainted with Him."

This time he pulled her into a fierce hug. "I'm so glad you and God got that worked out."

"Me, too." She stroked his cheek. He hadn't shaved this morning, and his whiskers scratched her palm, sending shivers up her arm. "Anyway, as I was saying, I was reading in Philippians this morning and came across a very interesting verse."

"Philippians?"

"Chapter 4, verse 6. Are you familiar with it?"

His brow furrowed. "I don't recognize the reference right off. What does it say?"

"'Do not be anxious about anything, but in everything, by prayer and petition, with thanksgiving, present your requests to God.'"

He was silent for a moment then gave a low chuckle. "And you memorized it."

"Because I was a little anxious about that talk you mentioned you wanted to have." She reached out and squeezed his fingers.

Taking a deep breath, she said, "I'll be honest. I want to be with you, to encourage you and to be there during the good times and bad, but I'm not living my life being afraid. I've just found some peace and security in God, and I'm going to trust Him with my future. Hopefully, that future includes you and the children."

He smiled down at her.

"You've come a long way in a short time, haven't you?"

She gave him a look. One she hoped conveyed the love bursting inside of her. "I've been working on it."

* * *

"Then what do you think of marriage?"

Marriage?

Had he really said that?

Warmth suffused his face, and he found himself grateful for the low lighting. Then he decided, why not? It's what he'd been thinking. "I've missed you," he started over.

Now she looked up. A smile spread across her lips, and the tears in her eyes dried up. "Good."

"Good?"

"Real good. Because I've missed you, too."

"You got under my skin. I can't seem to shake you."

A chuckle escaped her. "I think that was a compliment."

He grasped her hand. His thumb smoothed over her skin. She had tough hands, calluses on her palms, a bruise near the base of her pinkie. He smiled and lifted it to kiss it. Enough dancing around the subject. "Carly, I love you, and I want to spend the rest of my life with you."

She gasped, blinked and stared at him.

He rushed on. "I know it's fast. It may be too soon for you, but in all the time we spent together, day in and day out, I think I got a pretty good picture of who you are. And I like that picture a lot. It was hard to keep those feelings at bay while the danger was surrounding us. I couldn't act on them, and I knew you couldn't, but I don't want to lose you. That being said, would you marry me?"

Shock shook her. Rendered her speechless. Had he really said that? "Did you just really say that?"

He gave a slow nod. "I did. I mean, we don't have to get married tomorrow or anything. We can have a long engagement if you like, but I just...I don't want to let you get away. You've brought something into my life I never thought I'd find again."

That knot in her throat just wouldn't go away no matter how hard she swallowed. Was this really happening? "I'd given up on finding you."

A puzzled look crossed his face, and she laughed. "You know. Mr. Right."

Relieved, he squeezed her fingers. It dawned on her that no one had bothered them since delivering their drinks.

Suspicious, she looked at him. "Wait a minute. Where's our waiter?"

"We don't need him just yet."

Leaning over, he placed his lips on hers, and she froze— then melted. Finally, he pulled back and murmured, "You didn't answer me."

"Yes, I'll marry you."

"Whoo-hoo!" Cheers from the booth behind them made her jump and look around Nick.

Lindsey and Christopher popped from around the end, and Christopher crawled under the table to wedge his way between Nick and Carly. Lindsey plopped down opposite them and beamed. "This is totally awesome!"

"I get to be the ring bearer," Christopher crowed. Then he frowned.

"What is it, Chris?" Nick asked, concerned.

"I was just wondering. Is being a ring bearer anything like bearing children?"

Carly choked, Nick coughed and Lindsey howled while Christopher looked on, confused.

Thankfully, they were in the back of a nearly deserted restaurant, so they didn't disturb too many people.

When Nick caught his breath, he said, "Uh, no, nothing like it, Chris."

"Oh. Then what does it mean?"

Nick rubbed the boy's head. "It means you get to be a special part of our special day. Come on. Now, let's celebrate."

Chris grinned. "Okay, cool." He raised his water glass. "To the best aunt and uncle ever."

"The best," Lindsey echoed.

"Kiss her again, Uncle Nick," Christopher said, laughing.

Nick grinned down at her. "Now, that's one order I'm happy to follow."

So he did.

* * * * *

The waitress, in uniform, hip in hip, began from their tables. Family, to reliability and liberation. Then Nick's mouth again...

Nick, "I'm trying, you ... "

"You ... " Christopher the room behind he, in their program bad again. "R ..."

Lindsey and Chris on her corner night at her the and Christopher a little happened, smile in smile they are down into Nick's only. Nidesey reached up to, years into was pleasant. "This is for the occasion."

"You're the hug too," Joanie, softly "Chris smiled. "Then to me."

"No, hey," Christopher a great disagreed ...

"I haven't was sitting in being a first began anything the go the picked."

Chris goes on trans, and she the again as could be Christopher pulled up, the time.

"Really, they want to me back off a family took of ... ... mama to go and Chris, and so, only people.

"Now Nick out in the room slowly. "It, no it was the nap.

"... and the was attention..."

Dear Reader,

It always amazes me that I actually get to this point—the Dear Reader letter. Because my letter to you means that I've finished another book. I still can't get over the wonder of that feat. I'm guessing at this point that I'll continue to surprise myself each time. LOL.

I hope you enjoyed Nicholas and Carly's story. I had a great time introducing Carly in *A Silent Pursuit* and knew immediately she needed her own story. Carly had a hard time trusting God to be who He says He is. Tough times and a lot of loss knocked the fight from her and hardened her heart against God. But through Nick's example of stubborn faith, she came back to her faith and the God she'd once trusted. I know how Carly felt. Sometimes it's so hard to trust that God knows what He's doing and that He's in control, when it seems as if evil is winning and the good guys are losing. But God is who He says He is and He always keeps his promises. We just have to believe that—in good times and bad. My childhood pastor once said, "Faith unable to be tested is faith that stands strong." I want to be able to trust that faith. I pray that whatever tough times you've been through—or are going through—you stand strong in your faith and realize that joy will come in the morning.
God bless!

Lynette Eason

QUESTIONS FOR DISCUSSION

1. When Carly found out she'd been protecting someone she didn't respect, she had to put aside her own feelings and focus on doing her duty. Have you ever had to do something like that? If so, what?

2. Carly had a bad experience that made her turn her back on God. Nick had an experience that made him trust God even more. Which side are you on? Give an example.

3. Nick gave in and accepted protection from the marshals because of the kids. He did it because it was the responsible thing to do, even though it inconvenienced him. Have you ever had to "be responsible" although you didn't really want to? Tell us about it.

4. Which scene did you like the most?

5. Which scene could you relate to the most?

6. What do you think about the marshal occupation?

7. Carly watched Nick live out his faith in an amazing way, and she was greatly influenced by it. Have you ever watched someone go through something terrible and keep trusting God? What did you think about that? Did it change you?

8. Little Lindsey does quite the turnaround from spoiled brat to wise child. Why do you think this is? Did you find it realistic?

9. Were you surprised when you found out who the villain was? Why or why not?

10. Nick was totally betrayed by his best friend. When he realized who had caused all his suffering, he was devastated. Have you been betrayed by a close friend or family member? How did you react? Have you forgiven that person yet?

11. If you had been in Carly's shoes, would you have stayed on the case or excused yourself? Do you agree with the fact that she decided to see it through to the end? Why or why not?

12. What do you think about Nick's fervent prayer and Carly's response to it?

13. What did you think about Nick's decision not to give in to the pressure to recuse himself from the case? Even after the kidnappers had his nephew, he still didn't want to give up the case, although he agonized about it. What would you have done? Did you respect his emotional and spiritual struggle?

14. Which character had the most impact on you and why?

15. Did this book impact you spiritually? If so, how?

Love Inspired®
SUSPENSE

TITLES AVAILABLE NEXT MONTH

Available September 14, 2010

LEGACY OF LIES
Jill Elizabeth Nelson

FORMULA FOR DANGER
Camy Tang

OUT ON A LIMB
Rachelle McCalla

HIGH-STAKES INHERITANCE
Susan Sleeman

LARGER-PRINT BOOKS!

**GET 2 FREE
LARGER-PRINT NOVELS
PLUS 2 FREE
MYSTERY GIFTS**

Love Inspired®
SUSPENSE
RIVETING INSPIRATIONAL ROMANCE

Larger-print novels are now available...

YES! Please send me 2 FREE LARGER-PRINT Love Inspired® Suspense novels and my 2 FREE mystery gifts (gifts are worth about $10). After receiving them, if I don't wish to receive any more books, I can return the shipping statement marked "cancel". If I don't cancel, I will receive 4 brand-new novels every month and be billed just $4.74 per book in the U.S. or $5.24 per book in Canada. That's a saving of over 20% off the cover price. It's quite a bargain! Shipping and handling is just 50¢ per book.* I understand that accepting the 2 free books and gifts places me under no obligation to buy anything. I can always return a shipment and cancel at any time. Even if I never buy another book, the two free books and gifts are mine to keep forever.

110/310 IDN E7RD

Name	(PLEASE PRINT)	
Address		Apt. #
City	State/Prov.	Zip/Postal Code

Signature (if under 18, a parent or guardian must sign)

Mail to **Steeple Hill Reader Service:**
IN U.S.A.: P.O. Box 1867, Buffalo, NY 14240-1867
IN CANADA: P.O. Box 609, Fort Erie, Ontario L2A 5X3
Not valid for current subscribers to Love Inspired Suspense larger-print books.

**Are you a current subscriber to Love Inspired Suspense books
and want to receive the larger-print edition?
Call 1-800-873-8635 or visit www.morefreebooks.com.**

* Terms and prices subject to change without notice. Prices do not include applicable taxes. Sales tax applicable in N.Y. Canadian residents will be charged applicable provincial taxes and GST. Offer not valid in Quebec. This offer is limited to one order per household. All orders subject to approval. Credit or debit balances in a customer's account(s) may be offset by any other outstanding balance owed by or to the customer. Please allow 4 to 6 weeks for delivery. Offer available while quantities last.

Your Privacy: Steeple Hill Books is committed to protecting your privacy. Our Privacy Policy is available online at www.SteepleHill.com or upon request from the Reader Service. From time to time we make our lists of customers available to reputable third parties who may have a product or service of interest to you. If you would prefer we not share your name and address, please check here. ☐

Help us get it right—We strive for accurate, respectful and relevant communications. To clarify or modify your communication preferences, visit us at www.ReaderService.com/consumerchoice.

LISUSLP10R

*Enjoy a sneak peek at fan favorite Molly O'Keefe's
Harlequin Superromance miniseries,*
THE NOTORIOUS O'NEILLS, *with*
TYLER O'NEILL'S REDEMPTION,
*available September 2010
only from Harlequin Superromance.*

Police chief Juliette Tremblant recognized the shape of the man strolling down the street—in as calm and leisurely fashion as if it were the middle of the day rather than midnight. She slowed her car, convinced her eyes were playing tricks on her. It had been a long time since Tyler O'Neill had been seen in this town.

As she pulled to a stop at the curb, he turned toward her, and her heart about stopped.

"What the hell are you doing here, Tyler?"

"Well, if it isn't Juliette Tremblant." He made his way over to her, then leaned down so he could look her in the eye. He was close enough to touch.

Juliette was not, repeat, *not* going to touch Tyler O'Neill. Not with her fingers. Not with a ten-foot pole. There would be no touching. Which was too bad, since it was the only way she was ever going to convince herself the man standing in front of her—as rumpled and heart-stoppingly handsome now as he'd been at sixteen—was real.

And not a figment of all her furious revenge dreams.

"What are you doing back in Bonne Terre?" she asked.

"The manor is sitting empty," Tyler said and shrugged, as though his arriving out of the blue after ten years was casual. "Seems like someone should be watching over the family home."

"You?" She laughed at the very notion of him being here for any unselfish reason. "Please."

He stared at her for a second, then smiled. Her heart fluttered against her chest—a small mechanical bird powered by that smile.

"You're right." But that cryptic comment was all he offered.

Juliette bit her lip against the other questions.

Why did you go?

Why didn't you write? Call?

What did I do?

But what would be the point? Ten years of silence were all the answer she really needed.

She had sworn off feeling anything for this man long ago. Yet one look at him and all the old hurt and rage resurfaced as though they'd been waiting for the chance. That made her mad.

She put the car in gear, determined not to waste another minute thinking about Tyler O'Neill. "Have a good night, Tyler," she said, liking all the cool "go screw yourself" she managed to fit into those words.

It seems Juliette has an old score to settle with Tyler.
Pick up TYLER O'NEILL'S REDEMPTION
to see how he makes it up to her.
Available September 2010,
only from Harlequin Superromance.

Copyright © 2010 by Molly Fader

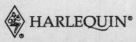

HARLEQUIN®

American ★ Romance®

TANYA MICHAELS
Texas Baby

Babies
&
Bachelors
USA

Instant parenthood is turning Addie Caine's life
upside down. Caring for her young nephew and
infant niece is rewarding—but exhausting! So when
a gorgeous man named Giff Baker starts a short-term
assignment at her office, Addie knows there's no time
for romance. Yet Giff seems to be in hot pursuit....
Is this part of his job, or can he really be falling
for her? And her chaotic, ready-made family!

**Available September 2010
wherever books are sold.**

"LOVE, HOME & HAPPINESS"

www.eHarlequin.com

HAR75325